UNSCROOGED

UNSCROOGED

W. Roy Weber

iUniverse, Inc.
Bloomington

UNSCROOGED

iUniverse books may be ordered through booksellers or by contacting:

iUniverse
1663 Liberty Drive
Bloomington, IN 47403
www.iuniverse.com
1-800-Authors (1-800-288-4677)

Because of the dynamic nature of the Internet, any web addresses or links contained in this book may have changed since publication and may no longer be valid. The views expressed in this work are solely those of the author and do not necessarily reflect the views of the publisher, and the publisher hereby disclaims any responsibility for them.

Any people depicted in stock imagery provided by Thinkstock are models, and such images are being used for illustrative purposes only.
Certain stock imagery © Thinkstock.

ISBN: 978-1-4620-4701-7 (sc)
ISBN: 978-1-4620-4703-1 (hc)
ISBN: 978-1-4620-4702-4 (ebk)

Printed in the United States of America

iUniverse rev. date: 10/07/2011

Contents

In memory of Lynda Silvester. Her *Letters, Sounds and Words* program and the Strong Start® Charitable Foundation will continue to make a difference in the lives of children. She has left a legacy of literacy to this country's young generation.

And to the dedicated members of Corporate Service Clubs, and Campus Service Clubs who give of their time for the betterment of the communities where they live, work and study.

Acknowledgments

I would like to thank my friends and family, who encouraged and supported me through the, sometimes, arduous task of writing this book. I would like to mention in particular my father-in-law, Don, who introduced me to the possibilities of publishing my work, as well as my brother-in-law, Alasdair, who provided a genuine perspective on the British way of life. Most of all I want to thank my wonderful wife, Heather, who was an endless source of support and encouragement as well as the best copy editor a husband could ask for.

My thanks would not be complete if I did not mention Second Cup. It was in the inviting surroundings of a Second Cup coffee house in Waterloo Ontario where I produced most of the writings for this book. I was inspired to create with a steaming cup of java by my side from the first word to my closing chapter.

Chapter 1

A Visit from Jacob

It was Jacob who had sent the three spirits. It was Jacob who had made it possible for Ebenezer to change before it was too late. And, it was Jacob who was now making his way up the frayed carpet stairs and through the door that led to Ebenezer's bedchambers. Ebenezer, dressed in his nightgown and cap, was seated snuggly in his fireside chair spooning the last bits of gruel from his bowl. Suddenly, Jacob appeared before him and without asking sat down in the empty chair next to his. Jacob was still as much a spirit as he was when Ebenezer had seen him just weeks before. Being a spirit, he was not of flesh and bone but a shadow-like replica of his human self. As humans, we change. We become fatter or thin. Hair is cut, or a beard is grown. A spirit, however, never changes. They are frozen in the image they bear the mystical instant they cease being. At least, that was what Ebenezer imagined to be true until seeing Jacob for a second time this night. Jacob was now invitingly different. Not in his overall appearance, though he still wore the same morning coat and starched collared shirt he was buried in. His hair was exactly no longer or shorter than it was before. It was not in his outward appearance, but in his countenance that he was different. Ebenezer could not describe it and scarcely believed it, but there was something different about Jacob, and he was more than interested in understanding what it was.

"My faithful friend, how good it is to feel your presence once again," Ebenezer said. Jacob was dragging a noticeably smaller length of chain.

"Your chain links, Jacob, there were once more of them than of you. What good fortune has manifested this change?"

1

"The last time I saw you, my chains carried the weight of my earthly transgressions. Each link was forged for every cruel word or selfish act I committed when I was alive. I was destined to carry these chains and feel the weight of my guilt for all eternity."

"Yes, this is what you told me, but I see now that you have far fewer links in your guilt-forged chain. Have you been absolved of your life's transgressions? Is this why you bear less of them?"

"It has begun, and it is to you, Ebenezer, that I owe my burden lightened."

"How could that be? After all, was it not I who benefited from your intervention?"

"Precisely, and your benefit has also become mine. For you gave rebirth to your once self-obsessed life by choosing to become a giving soul. You now have a generous heart filled to overflowing with a concern for the well-being of others. And since your change came from my doing, I too have been granted a chance at a new beginning."

"But you still appear as a wandering spirit. What new beginning is in that?"

"Because I was able to effect a change in you, Ebenezer, it may be possible that I will no longer be left to only watch the misery and cruelty that spans the earth, but will acquire the power to intervene and help restore the lives of the broken-hearted. You have given me hope for a re-birth of my own."

"So that is it. That is why you appear anew. Your burdens of guilt are being lifted for the good you did for me. What must happen now for your hope to be fulfilled?"

"Because of your newfound spirit of generosity, every good act of the heart you extend to another will help reduce each link of this chain I forged in life. However, in order for me to possess the power to intervene in the lives of the living and cast off all of my remaining chains, you must influence the change of heart in another living soul just as I did for you."

"So I must find someone whose heart is as hard as mine was and help them to cast off their selfish ways?"

"Yes, you must if I am to have any hope of releasing the celestial bond that holds me back from possessing the power to intervene in the lives of the living."

"I will do that for you, my good friend, Jacob. It is the least I can do after what you have done for me."

"There is just one condition that must be met in order for this power to be released to me."

"Whatever it is, I do pray it is within my control to comply."

"You must find this one earthly soul, and their heart must be transformed within no more than a year from the moment your heart was transfigured. It must, therefore, be before midnight on Christmas Eve of this very year."

"And what will happen if I am unable to find and save this lost soul by then?"

"Then I must remain as I am; a spirit that walks through this world as a witness to its misery but without the power to intervene in its healing."

"I will scan the world tenfold if I must to find just one whose heart can be changed. If I must do this by year's end, there is no time to lose. I will begin my quest at daybreak tomorrow."

"Thank you, my dear Ebenezer. Remember now that all you do until your last breath on earth will follow you into your life beyond this one. Every good deed of yours will be counted as a reward that awaits you there. Each act of kindness will be like a jewel added to your crown of compassion that will be yours to claim. I must leave you now. I do not know if I will see you again, but I will know each time you have extended a helping hand or uttered a word of encouragement to your neighbour by the lessening of my chains. Continue in the way you have, Ebenezer. Find just one whose heart is as hard as yours was and guide them as the Christmas spirits guided you. There will be no greater reward than to have those who have been changed by your good deeds with you that day in paradise."

Before Ebenezer could respond, Jacob vanished. He sat for a moment frozen in the silence of his room. He held his bowl in his hand for what seemed like an hour before he realized that he had not moved since Jacob disappeared. He placed the bowl on the edge of the hearth and gazed at a heap of ambers glowing in the fireplace, pondering what had just happened. Had he truly been able to transform the condition of Jacob's earth-bound spirit by the transformation of his own heart? Could one man's actions ripple in the lives of others like a pebble tossed on a stagnant pond? As he considered these matters, his mind came alive to the possibilities of what his actions could command. Then his thoughts began to race with ideas of people and places. What good could he build into the lives of those in this life who were drowning in despair, and who would it be whose heart he would help to transform? These thoughts of goodwill that he once scoffed at as a hard-hearted business man were now becoming familiar to him. He knew that there was so much he could do that he could scarcely keep himself from going back out into the streets of London that very night to begin his welcomed task. As he continued to envision the multitudes he was to give his tender care to, Jacob's words echoed in his ears.

"There will be no greater reward than to have those who have been changed by your good deeds with you that day in paradise."

What was this paradise Jacob was speaking of? And, what was awaiting him there? These mysterious words of Jacob's were the last thoughts that raced through his mind as he found himself fading into a slumber. The surprise of Jacob's visit and the excitement of all the possibilities of the good he could do for others had exhausted his last breath of the day. But tomorrow was a new day. Tomorrow he would begin his quest of finding that one soul's heart to transform, and in doing so, give to Jacob what only he had the earthly power to bestow.

Chapter 2

Mrs. Nottingham's Children

The clock on the mantel chimed seven times. A new day had begun with its morning light struggling through the soot-covered panes of his chamber windows. It shone on Ebenezer's face, forming around him a warm glow. It was the warm feel of the sunlight and not the chiming clock that awoke him.

Before thoughts of his own cares of the day entered his awakened mind, Ebenezer found himself engaged in thinking about others. The first person that he reflected on was, perhaps, the one who knew him the best. Mrs. Nottingham, his housekeeper, had given Ebenezer thirty years of her working life attending to his daily needs. By six each morning she was at her post to begin the tasks of the day. They began with the gathering of Ebenezer's soiled affairs, which he had placed in a hamper outside his bedroom chamber the night before. Next to the hearth stood the empty bowl of gruel that was Ebenezer's nightly ritual. With her arms filled with his personal effects, she would make her way down to the pantry. There she would unload her bundle to be attended to later in the day. She had a more important task to attend to—Ebenezer's morning meal.

Ebenezer was a man of habitual order. Each morning after attending to his grooming and dressing, he would come to sit at the dining table to have exactly the same breakfast—two soft-boiled eggs placed in an oval serving dish, two pieces of day-old bread toasted with a light brushing of butter, and a steaming cup of Earl Grey tea. The tea had to bear the mark of Earl Grey and no other. The Earl was a business acquaintance and political friend of Ebenezer's. He had financed the launch of the tea import enterprise that bore the Grey family name. The rise of the tea trade in England had made many shrewd businessmen rich, and Ebenezer was no exception. In preparation for his breakfast Mrs. Nottingham would pluck two freshly laid eggs from the roost of one of a dozen hens housed in the livery yard shed. The eggs had to be boiled for exactly five minutes in order to cook to the silky consistency Ebenezer was accustomed to.

This morning Mrs. Nottingham was slightly ahead of schedule. The breakfast was prepared and set on the table ready for Ebenezer's consumption before his expected arrival. She took the opportunity to make herself a smidgen to eat, something she normally wouldn't do until her noontime break. She sat on a worn wooden stool by the butcher's block in the middle of the kitchen. Just as she was bowing her head to whisper grace, Ebenezer burst in from the dining room service door.

"What a crisp winter morning it is, Mrs. Nottingham," Ebenezer exclaimed with a clap of his hands. Ebenezer was so preoccupied in greeting her that he did not notice that he was interrupting her prayer.

"My, Mr. Scrooge, you are up early on such a chilly morn." She was not bothered that Ebenezer had interrupted her without noticing; she knew that he had not done so intentionally.

"There is not a moment to lose of the day, Mrs. Nottingham. I have much work ahead, but first I must take my fill to give fuel to my activities. Please come join me in the dining room. We shall break bread together."

Mrs. Nottingham was not prepared for this invitation from Ebenezer. Although she was quickly coming to know him as a kind and gentle man, there was still the protocol between servant and master that dictated certain behavior. She reluctantly followed behind him as he pushed open the swinging door leading into the dining room. The plate of eggs and buttered toast was now cold from sitting too long. She was concerned that there would be stern criticism regarding the state of his breakfast. The former Ebenezer would have most certainly spit a bitter word of distain. She had forgotten that this new, gentler man would react in a different way. He, in fact, barely stopped to taste what was placed before him.

He was more interested in asking questions of Mrs. Nottingham. He began by asking about her children. How old were they, and how were they doing in school? Did they have enough to eat and proper clothes to wear? When he was told that the Nottinghams could not afford to send their children to school past the fourth level and that they were all, with the exception of the youngest boy, in child-labour factories, Ebenezer reacted with as much concern as a devoted grandparent would.

"It saddens me that your children are forced to work at such a tender age. They should be chasing rainbows, not toiling in workhouses," he cried. These thoughts would not have ever entered his mind just a few short weeks earlier. Rather he would be looking at the investment opportunity that existed in businesses that exploited the low cost of child labour. Children would have been faceless numbers on a ledger page. Now these numbers had faces. They had faces and hearts and souls. They were sons and daughters, brothers and sisters, friends and family. Ebenezer's heart welled up with such emotion that he began to weep. All he could see in his mind's eye were the sweat-covered faces of Mrs. Nottingham's children toiling in dreadful working conditions.

"Oh please, Mr. Scrooge. It is quite all right. All my children are fed and clothed and in good health," Mrs. Nottingham said, trying to dismiss the harsh reality that had become her existence.

"No, my dear Mrs. Nottingham, it is not at all right that your children are relegated to working for the rest of their lives. They are still children. They should be free to run and play, to laugh and discover. Instead they are treated like a cog in a wheel, and their existence only benefits the greedy owners and shareholders of these diabolical holes of industry."

"It has become all that we and our children know. At least where they are they are treated fairly. They are not beaten."

"As far as you know. There is nothing fair about any of this. They should not be anywhere near these factories. They should be filling their minds with wonder and knowledge. They should be in school, not shoveling coal."

"We do not have the means to put them into a school. That all costs money, and we depend on their income to help us to survive."

"You shall have the means. Consider this a benefit of your loyalty to me for all the years of dedicated service. I will cover any of the costs for putting your children into a proper school and compensate you for their lost wages."

"I could not accept such generosity, Mr. Scrooge. How could I ever pay you back?"

"You have paid me back in so many ways without my slightest acknowledgment. Consider this a long overdue wage increase. Now I want you this very hour to go and remove all of your dear sweet children from those workhouses. If their employer gives you any trouble, then tell them they will have Ebenezer Scrooge to contend with. I hold many of the mortgage papers on the commercial properties in London. They will know who I am. They will not want to cross me. If anyone refuses your request I will deal with it myself. Then bring them here and fill all the tubs and basins I have with hot steaming water. Give them each a thorough scrub. Meanwhile I will pay a visit to my tailor and instruct him to come swiftly and measure them for a new wardrobe. They are each to receive two Sunday bests and three sets of play clothes. We can't forget the play clothes. Their entire childhood must be returned to them, Mrs. Nottingham." Tears of joy began to stream down her tired face. She had long buried the feelings of the deep despair that overwhelmed her whenever she thought about her children.

"I just don't know how to thank you, Mr. Scrooge," she wept.

"There is no need to thank me, my dear woman. It is I who should thank you for serving me all these years while I never once gave you a word of gratitude or a raise in your wages."

The mention of money struck an immediate chord with Ebenezer. Money once had complete control over his life. Money was his god. It had given him his sense of worth and power. Money never disappointed him. It had never rejected him. Money allowed him to ignore his social morals. He had built a strongbox around his heart to keep all his money in and the love and concern of others out. But, now money was beginning to lose its grip on him. It was becoming what God had intended it to be: a tool to serve the needs of others. Ebenezer smiled as he reached for his hat and scarf hanging on the hall tree near the front entrance.

"Remember—go fetch all your children straightaway. I am off to my tailor. He will be here within the hour with his measuring tape and pincushion!" With his hat in hand and his scarf wrapped just once loosely around his neck, Ebenezer set off to call upon his tailor at the shop on the way to his offices. As he walked the narrow streets beginning to fill with the bustle of people, he could not put out of his mind the thought of the Nottingham family. How many countless other children were laboring in the mines, factories, and workhouses across England? Ebenezer was unaware that his newfound concern was about to lead to something significant. And it had all started with his caring question about his housekeeper's children. He was also unaware that at that moment a small coil of chain links appeared on the chair where he had sat having breakfast with Mrs. Nottingham. Jacob's chain of guilt had just become shorter.

Chapter 3

Covent Gardens

A narrow cobblestone alley opened up into a grand market square. It was a buzz of activity, as it always was in the early hours of the day. It had first been a tract of land used for a monastery's provisional garden, but when Henry the VIII abolished the Catholic Church's ownership of land in England it was sold to a wealthy merchant who developed the property as a place of commerce and trade. It was this history that gave it the name of Covent Gardens.

A host of merchants were plying their wares to the attentive customers buying for their daily needs. There were carts and long tables full to overflowing with fresh local and imported produce. Bulging heads of cauliflower and broccoli, fat turnips, stocky potatoes, and plump, ripe tomatoes painted a picture of bounty. There were crates of pineapples, oranges, and green bananas that looked like they had just arrived from the dry docks. They would have come from never-before-seen places like Antigua, Fiji, and Zanzibar. It was a sight to behold. Ebenezer was amazed at all the colours and aromas that surrounded him. He had passed this way every working day of his adult life, but for the first time he really saw, and noticed, all the astonishing detail in everything around him. It was the minute design of the commonest of things that gave him pleasures—an apple, for instance. He had never noticed the shining red skin of it before. How smooth and round it felt in the palm of his hand. He had never thought to smell one, but today he found himself taking interest with a sense of wonder. It was as if he was discovering his world all over again. This time he was becoming aware of the abundance and beauty that was found in all of creation. When one's heart is turned to stone there is no feeling left to give, even to benefit one's own wellbeing. Ebenezer's hardness of heart, which blocked him from feeling anything for humanity, had also blocked him from caring about anything else. Before, food to him was only viewed as a necessary element to survive. The fact that eating a meal took time out of his work schedule annoyed him. The only reason green grocers had ever interested him before was if he had any business trading with them. Ebenezer approached the vendor, Mr. Cooper, with the prized fruit in his hand.

"This apple has to be the most beautiful work of nature I have ever seen. Wouldn't you agree?" Ebenezer asked.

"Sure, I sell dozens of those beautiful works of nature every day!" Mr. Cooper laughed.

"You are surrounded by this beauty every day. How fortunate you are." Ebenezer replied. He polished the apple on his jacket and then rotated it to catch the sunlight.

"See the way it shines?"

"So does the half pence it will cost you," replied Mr. Cooper, chuckling to himself.

"So it will. Perhaps I can find more than a half pence if you would be willing to sell me the lot."

"And how much would the lot be worth to you?" quipped Mr. Cooper.

"What value can you put on the smile on a child's face? I intend to surprise a family who I know could never afford one apple, never mind your whole lot." Ebenezer was thinking of a poor family he knew of who lived close by his counting house. The father was a chimney sweep who struggled to keep his wife and six children fed and clothed.

Suddenly, Mr. Cooper recognized Ebenezer.

"I have seen you pass by here before, but you never stopped to buy. You look like Mr. Scrooge—Ebenezer Scrooge, the businessman. But, that can't be. You are far too charitable."

Very few knew of Ebenezer's recent change. They knew him only as he was, a self-serving old man with a life maligned with solitude. Any kind act or word from the former Ebenezer Scrooge was no more expected than a rose blooming in the dead of winter. It would not be long, however, before the word of Ebenezer's transformation was on the lips of all the citizens of London. It would be fodder for neighbourhood pub jabbering and fuel to stock the gossip at afternoon teas all across the city.

"I am he," smiled Ebenezer as he extracted his purse from his jacket pocket to pay for his purchase. As Mr. Cooper was exchanging the apples for the six-pence payment, out of the crowd a hand snatched Ebenezer's purse, and the thief ran off with it, disappearing across the busy square.

"That little street thief is at it again," shouted Mr. Cooper. "I have had too many customers robbed by that no good, I tell you. No one wants to buy from me when they don't feel safe."

"So you know who just stole my purse?" asked Ebenezer.

"I know who it is as sure as I'm standing here selling you these apples, I do. His name is Tobias Harding. His father was killed in a coal mine accident, and his mother—well, I'm not sure where she is. She could be dead too for all I know. All I do know is that he has been on the streets picking pockets to survive for some three years now. Every time it happens we call for a bobby; then he's found and put back into the stockades. Can you watch me stall for just a minute?" asked Mr. Cooper.

With that he shot across the square, dodging pedestrians as he made his way to a police officer he noticed standing at his street station.

"He's up to it again, Constable. That Harding boy just lifted Mr. Scrooge's purse filled with pound sterling. He made off in the direction of the river-barge loading docks down by Victoria Embankment. Shall I instruct Mr. Scrooge to come over to Scotland Yard to claim his property?" he asked.

"If he's in his usual hideout it won't take us long. But, just in case, give us an extra day. Tell Mr. Scrooge to come by the station tomorrow," replied the constable. When Mr. Cooper returned to his stall, he relayed to Ebenezer exactly what was instructed to him.

"I have been to court countless times to put many of my tenants into debtor's prison, but never have I been there myself. It must be a horrible place, and this young Tobias will likely be a permanent resident there unless he is given a chance to change his ways. I would like to help this poor boy. I am sure he has a story of troubles that has caused his decline into crime."

"But that poor boy just stole from you, Mr. Scrooge. I know his kind; they never change. I don't think you or anyone else can help someone like that," Mr. Cooper replied with skepticism.

"You and I are people whom God has blessed with all we need to live and lead a productive life. There are many to whom this grace has yet to be extended, so we must give hope to the hopeless and kindness to those who seem least deserving of it."

"If only we all could do as you desire, Mr. Scrooge, this world would be a kinder place."

"We can all do what is good and right. What we desire in our hearts can become what we desire to do. All it takes is our will. You said that the constable wanted me to wait until tomorrow to see him about Tobias?"

"Yes, he needs time to hunt the boy down and bring him in. You can pass by the station tomorrow. They should have rounded him up by then."

"Rounded him up? He is not a herded animal. He is a young lad who has had a tough go of life. He needs a second chance, and I'm the one who is going to give it to him."

"So you won't be pressing charges, then?" Mr. Cooper asked with a tone of disbelief.

"He has been charged enough before, and that did nothing to help him to reform his ways. He will be given a clean slate and a chance to restart his life. I was given such a chance myself, and I am a new man because of it."

"I dare say you are, Mr. Scrooge. If I didn't know you by appearance, I would claim you to be an imposter. For the way you act toward others is so completely opposite to your old self, I can only believe that your spirit has been reborn, and you along with it. If Ebenezer Scrooge can change like this, then any one of us can do the same. You have shown me today that it is possible to begin me life again a new person."

"I stand here as a testimony that anyone, even a hard-hearted old man like I was, can change."

"Well, if Ebenezer Scrooge can do it, then there is hope for all of us. You have even convinced me that I might be able to change me self," replied Mr. Cooper. He finished putting the rest of his lot of apples in a burlap sack.

"It's been a pleasure to serve you today, Mr. Scrooge."

"Please, call me Ebenezer."

"Ebenezer, please call me Ben. Ben Cooper is me name." He extended his right hand to shake Ebenezer's, holding the sack of apples in his left.

"You will, no doubt, see more of me, Ben."

"It is a pleasure to call you a valued customer, Ebenezer."

Ebenezer took the sack and flung it over his shoulder. He was anxious to deliver the apples to their intended family. His desire to give unselfishly to others was growing fervently in him. When he was a young business apprentice and attended church, he had heard the preacher say that it was more blessed to give than to receive. He remembered how foolish that sounded and thought that if one was to ever get ahead in the world they had to think of themselves first. It may have been a blessed thing to give rather than to receive, but it certainly was not profitable. He never went to church again after hearing that. The transformed Ebenezer, however, now knew it to be true. There is an inexplicable joy that one experiences when they give expecting nothing in return.

Ebenezer bid good-bye to Mr. Cooper and continued on his way. As he walked down the street toward his office, he heard a faint pinging sound behind him, but he did not see the chain link that had landed under Mr Cooper's fruit cart.

Before arriving at his counting house, Ebenezer remembered to stop by his tailor's shop. The sign over the door had the name "Weaver" on it with an etched symbol that looked like a spool of thread and a needle. Ebenezer opened the door to a small workshop lined with bolt upon bolt of woven cloth. In the back, Mr. Weaver was bent over a sewing table, working only by the light that streamed through the small shop window. "Good morning, Mr. Weaver, and how are you this fine winter day?" Ebenezer asked with a lively smile.

"Each day is a gift from above, Mr. Scrooge. I have never been given a gift I would return," replied Mr. Weaver.

"You have a fine attitude about life. It is an attitude that will make the difference between a life just endured and one lived with purpose."

"You speak the truth, my good sir. So what is your purpose today?"

"I am here not on my own affair but that of my housekeeper, Mrs. Nottingham, or should I say that of her five children."

Ebenezer continued by explaining and directing Mr. Weaver to bring the very best and durable bolts of cloth and the strongest of threads to stitch pants, skirts, shirts, and jackets for Mrs. Nottingham's children.

"Remember, Mr. Weaver, that these clothes, especially the play clothes, must withstand the most vigorous of activity. These deserving children have a mountain of time to make up for in being carefree and boundless in their youthful discovery. These outfits will get a lot of wear, so you'd best reinforce the knees and elbows," he instructed with a smile in his eyes.

"They will have to play a lifetime to wear out my handiwork, Mr. Scrooge," replied Mr. Weaver.

"That is what I like to hear. Mrs. Nottingham is expecting you. You know where to go."

With that he turned and walked out the door. As he continued along toward his counting house, he was so preoccupied with pondering the fate of this Tobias Harding that he did not notice that he had passed the entrance to his office. He was already ten steps beyond before he realized his oversight. He backtracked to the counting house entrance, and as he reached for the doorknob the door swung open with a great thrust from the other side.

"Master Peter, it is good to see you ready to take on the world this morning with such vigor. Where are you off to?"

"Good morning to you, Mr. Scrooge. So sorry for startling you, but I must go and see my little brother in hospital—the very hospital you arranged for him."

"And how is our Tiny Tim?"

"He is doing so well. They say he may soon be able to walk without his crutch."

"Now that is good news! I must tell your father to bring him home for a visit, and we can all see him. It makes my heart sing to see how he is doing so well."

"It has all been thanks to your generosity, Mr. Scrooge. Without you, he would surely not live long."

"My dear boy, it is not me but by the grace of God."

"Well then, thank God for giving you such a generous heart, sir. Please tell father I shall not be too long in returning. There is a great deal of work to complete before the end of the day," stated Peter.

"The work will always be there, but time with your family will not. You take your time, and make sure you tell Tim he is always in our hearts and minds," Ebenezer countered warmly.

"No need to tell him that, Mr. Scrooge. He surely knows he is loved, especially by you."

"Nevertheless, do tell him, will you?"

"Without fail, I will!" assured Peter.

As he entered the office, he saw Bob Cratchit busily working on the ledger books that held the inner workings of Ebenezer's enterprise. He had made Bob his office administrator and put him in charge of all matters that pertained to his vast business interests. The old Ebenezer would trust nothing of his financial matters to anyone, least of all his office clerk, Bob Cratchit. Not only had he promoted Bob, but he had also raised his pay tenfold. Bob could now provide well for his family. Ebenezer's generosity didn't end there. He had also engaged Bob's son, Peter, as an apprentice office clerk. Peter was given quite a decent wage for his position, with opportunity for advancement as good as guaranteed.

"Good morning to you, Bob. Your Peter is such a fine young gentleman. He is as conscientious and enterprising as his father. He will go far here, under his father's wise guidance."

"Thank you, Mr. Scrooge. You have given both us Cratchits the key to prosperity."

"Now, Bob, how many times have I told you to call me Ebenezer? You are my trusted manager, and you should be free to speak to me as your peer."

"I am sorry. It has been difficult for me to address you that way . . . Ebenezer. I did not even remember your first name before you began requesting I use it. I have always known you as sir, or Mr. Scrooge."

"Oh my, that is amusing. You didn't even remember my first name? I wonder how many others not as close to me as you have been don't know my first name? Well, I want it to be Ebenezer to all my adult acquaintances from here in. Now I must say it is great news to hear your Tim is coming along. We must gather the family and celebrate his continued recovery. How about this Sunday? We can all come to my home, or perhaps Tim would be more comfortable in his own surroundings?"

"Yes, that is a fine idea. Mrs. Cratchit will cook her goose and dumplings."

"Oh how I love Mrs. Cratchit's dumplings smothered in her thick gravy. You are a fortunate man, Bob, to have such a wife. No wonder your stomach is twice the size of mine." he laughed.

The office had become a place of fellowship and good tidings. An unexpected result for Ebenezer was that his business had begun to increase and profits had multiplied. He had not planned it that way. He had simply started paying more attention to relationships rather than the ledger page. It was more important to see that his staff and business associates were considered not for what they could do for him but for what he could do for them. This servant attitude had resulted in an outpouring of prosperity for Ebenezer. He had been a man of great financial means before, but now he was becoming a man of significance.

Chapter 4

His Day in Court

Ebenezer awoke with one thing on his mind. The thief of his purse was, by now, in the jailhouse awaiting a judge's sentence. As the victim of this crime, Ebenezer was the only one who could do anything to amend the boy's fate. His sentence would, most likely, be harsh and without mercy. Ebenezer had been told this was not his first violation and that he had been in jail many times. With Ebenezer's position as a prominent businessman, the crown would likely want to set an example and request the maximum penalty for this offense. English law and its judgments could be severe. Ebenezer was determined for this not to happen to Tobias. He would intervene and appeal to the judge on behalf of the boy. With this in mind, Ebenezer quickly dressed and forwent his usual breakfast, taking only a dry piece of toast on his way out the door to the courthouse square.

He had determined where the court was and how he was to make his way there. It would only take him a few minutes by foot—a good thing as it was now drawing close to eight o'clock and Tobias's case was due to begin. He arrived, according to his pocket watch, three minutes before the hour. It was a dull building faced with rough-cut stone that gave the impression of strict authority. It was attached to the police station where Tobias had spent the night locked up. As he entered the building he noticed an official-looking uniformed man sitting at a raised oak desk. He was filling out papers while referring to his watch continuously.

"Could you be so kind and direct me to where Tobias Harding is being judged?" Ebenezer asked, hoping he was indeed in the right place.

"You mean that street dog jailed for pinching the purse of Mr. Scrooge?" the man replied. He was the duty clerk responsible for scheduling the list of the twenty-eight judgments that day, and he was busy at work juggling the courtroom bookings with the judges available.

"The judge is bound to throw that one away for good today. A man like Mr. Scrooge surely will want his restitution. That boy picked the wrong man to steal from, don't you think?"

"Well, it could be that Mr. Scrooge may want to help this young lad and give him the chance to turn his life around."

"Help this young lad? Do you know who Mr. Scrooge is? He is not one to let anyone off the hook or lend them a helping hand; no indeed, not him."

"I must disagree with you, sir. I believe that Mr. Scrooge will do exactly that. He is going to see to it that Mr. Harding is given the one chance he deserves to reform himself and redeem his sordid past."

"And who might you be?"

"I, my good man, am Ebenezer Scrooge, your humble servant."

"Oh, now I must say that is the best one I have heard all week. So you are Ebenezer Scrooge, are you? And I am King William IV."

Just as the duty clerk said this, a man walked in wearing a stained canvas apron. It was Mr. Cooper, the fruit merchant whom Ebenezer had just met the day before.

"Good morning, Mr. Scrooge. You must be here for the sentencing. I was called as a witness. I do hope this don't take too long. I had to leave me stall and me customers to come here."

The duty clerk blushed with embarrassment as he realized that, in fact, it was Ebenezer he had been speaking with.

"I am sorry, Mr. Scrooge. I didn't mean to be disrespectful."

"No harm done, my good man. Now that we have settled that, Mr. Cooper and I do need to know where Tobias Harding's judgment is convening."

The duty clerk rifled through his scheduling papers to find the room.

"They are in the Wellington chamber, down the hall and first door on the right. It is Judge Bartholomew's courtroom. That should make for an interesting session."

"Please tell me. What do you mean by interesting?" asked Ebenezer with a tone of concern in his voice.

"Judge Bartholomew has a reputation for giving harsh sentences, especially to repeat offenders like your Tobias Harding. He is known as Bang-Bang Bartholomew. The bang referring to his judge's gavel striking the desk as he pronounces the sentence."

"I appreciate your insight, Mr.—?"

"James Banks. Pleased to meet you, Mr. Scrooge."

"The pleasure is all mine, Mr. Banks. And thank you again for all your assistance this morning. You are a faithful servant to the people of London," replied Ebenezer.

With no time to lose, Ebenezer and Mr. Cooper scrambled down the hall to find the Wellington chamber. As they turned the corner they saw a procession entering what had to be the room they were looking for. At the front walked a short man robed in an oversized black gown. He wore a white, wavy-haired wig that rested just above his shoulders. Behind him marched a young man carrying a large leather-bound book, and behind him followed two more black-gowned men wearing similar wigs to the man who must have been the judge presiding over the court. Behind all of them Ebenezer noticed Tobias with his hands bound behind his back being led by a jail guard. Ebenezer and Mr. Cooper followed the procession into the chamber, closing the door behind them. Before they could sit down, one of the two black-gowned men approached them.

"May I ask which of you is Mr. Benjamin Cooper?"

"I am Benjamin Cooper. I trust you are the prosecutor, then? Tell me, how long will this little issue take? I'm losing me income by being here and need to make this hasty," Mr. Cooper added with a tone of frustration.

"I thank you for coming this morning, Mr. Cooper. I do appreciate that you have left your business unattended to come and testify. The crown will recognize your loss in serving the public and compensate you with a half crown for your trouble," replied Mr. Jenks, the crown prosecutor.

"Well that is a fine thing. It don't hurt as much now, I must say."

Mr. Cooper smiled as he made his way to the witness box. Without warning, the young man who had carried in the leather-bound book stood up and announced in a loud, monotone voice, "Judge Bartholomew presiding. This is the case of the people versus Tobias Harding. Let the record show that the accused is being judged according to the King's common law, and all rulings are binding without appeal."

Ebenezer had heard this statement a thousand times before, but never had he realized the severity of the words. All rulings are binding without appeal. Tobias was given only one chance to make his case and face one man's final judgment. Today that man was Judge Bartholomew. He looked unassuming sitting behind his massive judicial desk that towered over the courtroom. Only his head and torso were visible from where Ebenezer was sitting. This made it look as if he had no legs or feet. He knew that Tobias must be feeling quite nervous and fearful as he stood directly in front of the witness box. From where Tobias was standing, the judge and his desk would have appeared daunting. If only Tobias could see the judge from Ebenezer's perspective, it would help him to see that Judge Bartholomew was no more daunting than a toad on an oversized stump.

"Would the crown and defending attorney please approach the bench," snapped Judge Bartholomew. Tobias' day in court had begun.

"It is the opinion of this court that the accused will receive a swift judgment as, according to his record, there have been numerous offenses filed against him, and it appears that he has shown no remorse or desire for rehabilitation from his actions."

"Although his criminal record is extensive, your lordship, we must be fair in judging each offense and allow it to stand on its own," replied Mr. Wordsworth, the attorney assigned to Tobias's case.

"I will determine what is and what is not fair in my courtroom, Mr. Wordsworth. Now let us proceed. Mr. Jenks, you may call your first witness."

Mr. Jenks was a young, and aspiring legal counselor who had graduated from Cambridge a short four years earlier. He was known for his persistent style and the ability to force the truth from any witness who was subjected to his unrelenting line of questioning.

"The crown calls Mr. Benjamin Cooper." As he said this he turned and looked directly at Mr. Cooper, who had been sitting in the witness box since entering the court. The court clerk had already sworn him in, so Mr. Jenks' questioning began without delay.

"Mr. Cooper, could you please tell the court what your occupation is?"

"I run a fruit and vegetable stall in Covent Garden. Have done for over twelve years now."

"And what did you see yesterday morning happen at your stall?"

"I was selling apples to Mr. Scrooge, Ebenezer Scrooge. He is right there in the gallery." Mr. Cooper pointed to Ebenezer as he replied to Mr. Jenks' question.

"Thank you, Mr. Cooper. Tell us what happened next."

"Just as Mr. Scrooge took out his change purse to pay for the apples, out of nowhere someone came up from behind and snatched it from his hands."

"Did you get a good look at the thief?"

"I did, sir. I saw him as plain as I see you standing there."

"Do you see the thief in this courtroom?"

"He's standing right there in the prisoner box."

"Let the record show that the witness has identified Tobias Harding, the accused. Thank you, Mr. Cooper. I have no further questions."

Judge Bartholomew then summoned Tobias's attorney to question the witness.

"Mr. Cooper, can you tell me how many fingers I am holding up?" Mr. Wordsworth raised his hand to show three fingers.

"Well, I would say you are holding up two fingers, or maybe three. No, I'm sure it is two."

"If it pleases the court, your lordship, may we consider this witness without integrity, as I have just shown he cannot see clearly four feet in front of himself?"

"That is not true. There is a difference between bony white fingers and the face of a thief; a thief I know not only by sight but also by his smell," interjected Mr. Cooper, defending his statement.

"Are you telling this court that you can identify my client by smell, Mr. Cooper?"

"A boy like that don't get to washing much, so it isn't long before he begin to . . . well, stink."

Ebenezer was troubled by the way Tobias was being spoken of. He was a human being and was worthy of respect like anyone else. We are not all given the same privileges in life. Our circumstances and the choices we make shape and form our lives. We are all individuals of worth, created in God's image. Ebenezer was now anxious to be on the witness stand so that he could express his sentiments and influence the outcome of Tobias's trial.

"This court cannot convict someone on the basis of their bodily odour. It is not distinct to that person; a similar odour could be shared by a number of people. Your lordship, I move that the testimony of Mr. Cooper be stricken as it is clear that his sight is suspect and therefore his testimony is not credible."

"I will sustain that motion reluctantly. I trust that you have another witness, Mr. Jenks, who can testify and who is not short of sight?"

"Yes, I do, your lordship. The people call Mr. Ebenezer Scrooge."

Ebenezer rose from his seat in the gallery and made his way to the witness box. This was his opportunity to alter the course of the trial and convince the judge to drop the charges against Tobias.

"Was it your purse that was stolen while you were standing in front of Mr. Cooper's stall yesterday, Mr. Scrooge?" asked Mr. Jenks with a confident, controlling tone.

"It was. Yes, no doubt about that," replied Ebenezer.

"And did you see the thief who stole it from you?"

"Yes, I did see him for a brief moment."

"Is he in this courtroom presently?"

"Well, I am not completely sure about that. It could be that boy standing in the prisoner box, but then again it may not. Perhaps I didn't get a clear enough look at him."

"Please take a good, long look at the accused, Mr. Scrooge. It is important that you recognize him in order to settle this and have your purse returned to you."

"Objection, your lordship. Mr. Jenks is leading the witness," interjected Mr. Wordsworth.

"Sustained. We will strike that last comment from the record."

With that, the court clerk took his pen and struck out what was last said to Ebenezer.

"But what if it doesn't matter to me if I get my purse back or not?" replied Ebenezer amidst the jockeying back and forth between the attorneys.

"I beg your pardon, sir. What did you just say?" asked the judge with slight disbelief.

"I said what if I don't care if I get it back. In fact, your lordship, I would like to drop the charges against this young man and ask the court's permission to take him on under my guardianship. I do believe that, as the victim, I have that right. Is that not so, your lordship?"

The judge looked rather perplexed, but with some hesitation he affirmed that he did have the right to drop the charges. The guardianship, however, would be yet another matter.

"I believe that this young man deserves some mercy and forgiveness for the deeds of his past. And since it was I who was

24

last affected and for whom we are here today, I request that your lordship grant me the right to vindicate him of his misdemeanor."

"I can grant you this, Mr. Scrooge, but I caution you that this boy has been a frequent visitor to this court, and he must be properly reformed otherwise he will continue to do wrong."

"And has his previous punishment done anything to reform him, your lordship?"

"Perhaps he needs a series of strict reminders in order to correct him, Mr. Scrooge."

"Perhaps he needs a different kind of reminder, your lordship. A kinder and gentler one."

"I welcome you to find that better way, Mr. Scrooge. As for his guardianship, may I suggest that you first see if he will respond to you. Take him home with you and begin your reform there. You will know soon enough whether you can bring the boy to his senses while he is living under your care. Come and see me when he has been with you a while, and if you are still desiring to be his guardian, I will make it so. But, I caution you, he is deceiving and crafty and is not to be trusted."

The judge slammed his gavel twice on the desk and then he rose, leaving the courtroom through a private passage behind his bench. Ebenezer was pleased to have been able to convince the judge that it would be best for Tobias to be with him. What happened next with Tobias he could not predict, but he knew in his heart that what he had just done was the right thing to do. He walked over to Tobias and introduced himself. Tobias seemed at ease with Ebenezer and quite willing to return home with him. No doubt he figured that any place had to be better than the cold cell he had just spent the night in. They left the courtroom talking and asking questions of each other. As they walked, it occurred to Ebenezer that Jacob had told him that any kind deed he extended to another would reduce the links of the chain he was forced to carry. He wondered how many links in Jacob's chain he had helped to remove this day. If he would have remained but a moment longer in the courtroom, he would have had his answer. Out of nowhere appeared a chain of four links. They fell and landed directly on the seat where Ebenezer had sat during the trial.

Chapter 5

Chesterfield Hill

Ebenezer grinned as Tobias stood staring all around the vestibule.

"I have never been in such a fine house as yours, Mr. Scrooge. Quite fancy, I should say."

"Well, Tobias, this is your home now, and everything is yours to request," replied Ebenezer, chuckling to himself.

"Everything?"

"You will have all that you need, Tobias. There will be enough for you to eat, and we'll get you some proper clothing fitting a young Englishman. And you will have the chance to know what good comes from earning an honest day's keep. Tomorrow morning I will take you to my counting house where you can begin work as one of my clerks. But right now we need to get some food into you and then get you cleaned up and settled into your quarters."

"Beg your pardon, Mr. Scrooge, but what are quarters? Is that a fancy name for a pair of pants?"

"No, it's not a piece of clothing, Tobias. It's just another word for a bedroom." Ebenezer smiled, realizing that Tobias was truly from another world. A world within a world; one about which he knew very little. Ebenezer figured they would learn a great deal from each other.

"And we have to figure out what you will call me. I think Mr. Scrooge is too formal, and Ebenezer is too familiar. You know, I feel like an uncle to you. You remind me of my nephew, Fred, who is my only living relative. He calls me Uncle Ebenezer. How does that sound to you? Would Uncle Ebenezer suit you?"

"I've never had an uncle before. If I did, I never knew him or he never would want it to be known that he was."

Tobias liked the idea of family, but Ebenezer wasn't family. His mother was his only family. Still, the house was better than the street regardless of whether he was or wasn't.

"I've always wanted to have family, and I like the idea of calling you my uncle. So Uncle Ebenezer it is. You know, with all this court business, I haven't been able to tell you how thankful I am that you saved me from goin' back to jail. I know you've taken a big risk hav'n me here and tak'n me in as family. I want you to know that I won't disappoint you, Mr. Scrooge—I mean Uncle Ebenezer."

For the first time in his life Ebenezer felt a pride that wasn't for himself or for his own efforts but for someone else. It felt as if Tobias was actually family, and he was feeling the pride a parent feels when their child exhibits good character.

"You know, Tobias, I don't know anything about the family you do have. Your mother—is she still living?"

"I wouldn't say she's living; barely surviving she is. Mum caught pneumonia a year back, and it has not gotten any better. She's quite sick and laid up in an infirmary down on Agars Street. It don't look good, not with the kind of care she gets in there. I'm afraid she won't survive much past the spring," Tobias answered with worry in his voice.

"A public infirmary, I'm afraid, is not a place for getting better. We'll work on a way to get your mother the proper care she needs," replied Ebenezer with concern.

"That's what I've been trying to do, but it takes more than I've got to get her into a proper hospital."

"If you are willing to let me help you, she will not stay where she is."

"She's all I've got. I'm all alone if she dies."

"We all have our designated time here on earth, Tobias, but we can help delay its coming. Don't you worry about that for now. Let's get you something to eat and a change of clothes. I'll go fetch Mrs. Nottingham to cook something up for you and find you something to wear." As Ebenezer said this, he was already contemplating what he could do for Tobias and his sick mother.

Ebenezer then went off to look for Mrs. Nottingham, leaving Tobias standing alone in the vestibule. He was still thinking about his mother. She had been his focus of attention for over a year now, and he was more than determined to see her brought back to health. Although he knew it was wrong to steal to meet his needs, he had felt great satisfaction after taking Ebenezer's purse. With the money that was in it, he could have finally paid to have his mother moved to a better place where she could begin to recover properly. Getting caught was a definite setback, and he could not help feel a certain resentment toward Ebenezer. He knew that this was not rational thinking, for it was Ebenezer who freed him from prison. But he continued to struggle with a sense of hopelessness and shortcoming in not being able to help his mother. He knew he had to trust Ebenezer to help get his mother out of the infirmary. He wanted to trust Ebenezer, but he could not yet bring himself to relinquish his self-reliance. This was a reliance that he had fought to build. It had defined who he was and kept him strong all the nights he spent on the streets of London. It was part of him when he was being chased by the law. It was with him the countless times he had to defend himself. The street is ruthless to a young man alone with only his raw and instinctive will to live. Tobias was determined that if he was to succeed at getting his mother out of that place where she lay dying, he would have to do it on his own. He began pondering ways to raise the needed funds. Perhaps there would be an opportunity at his new workplace. Ebenezer would be taking him there tomorrow. He knew nothing about the dealings of Ebenezer's counting house; only that in counting houses there was money. As he thought about it, a sly grin appeared on his face. Tobias had a good inkling that he would find what he needed there. Tomorrow he would know it for certain.

Chapter 6

The Junior Clerk

The morning came early to Tobias. He was habitually late in rising, not usually before noon. He would be out most nights well past midnight. Sometimes he would be out all night prowling the dark streets of London. It was at night when he did most of his trade and thievery. On this day, a beam of morning light streamed in through the window of his bedroom, blinding him and making him squint to see the time on the clock that stood on the fireplace mantel. It showed that it was ten minutes past seven. On the chair beside the fireplace he noticed a shirt and pair of pants that weren't there the night before. Mrs. Nottingham must have placed them there after he had gone to bed. He instinctively jumped out of his bed and ran to inspect them. As he pulled the shirt over his head, he smelled a scent that he had never smelled before. It was the scent of new clothes, clothes that had never been worn before by anyone else. These were his own clothes; new clothes that fit him exactly. He tried on every piece until he was completely dressed from shirt to shoes. How soft and crisp they were. His shirt was well starched with long cuffs that seemed to stretch to his knuckles. The pants were cuffed exactly to ride on the tops of the black leather shoes that fit him like bedroom slippers. Tobias had never been given anything like this before. He had begged for or stolen anything he had ever possessed. For the first time in his life, he was beginning to experience feelings of thankfulness. He was confused as to whether he was feeling thankful or beholding. Never had he received something without there being an expectation of him having to do or give something in return. He sensed that Ebenezer had given him these things as a gift and expected nothing in return. But his street-hardened skepticism kept him from fully trusting these newfound feelings. For now, he would simply accept the fact that he had been given a new set of clothing, a new home to live in, and a new job that would keep him off the streets.

"Master Tobias, you'd best be up and dressed and down here for breakfast," chirped Mrs. Nottingham from the vestibule.

"I'm coming," Tobias replied as he made his way to the top of the staircase.

"The master has already come down and finished his. You'd best be quick so as not to keep him waiting to leave," said Mrs. Nottingham in a motherly tone. Tobias came bursting into the dining room, nearly taking the swing door off its hinges.

"Good morning, Tobias, and how did you sleep your first night in your own bed?" asked Ebenezer, sitting at the head of the table wiping the last crumb of his breakfast from the corner of his mouth.

"It was the best sleep I've ever had; like sleeping on a bed of feathers," Tobias replied.

"That is because it was. Most mattresses are either filled with straw or horse hair, but there are some that have the soft, sinking feel of goose feathers. The pillows are filled with them as well," Ebenezer chuckled.

"It'll be difficult to get up every morning with such a bed."

"No problem. Mrs. Nottingham will make sure you are up and dressed to be at work by eight o'clock every morning. Speaking of work, we leave in five minutes, so you'd best eat quickly!" Ebenezer insisted.

Ebenezer had become, indeed, a kinder man, but he still maintained a firm work ethic. There was a time for work and a time for leisure, but now work time was often eclipsed by time with others and with enjoying life's simple pleasures. The two were at the front door ready to depart within minutes. Tobias was eager to start his first day at work. He was told that he would be working directly with Peter Cratchit, Bob's son, who was now a senior clerk. Tobias felt both excited and apprehensive. It was the kind of excitement that one feels when adventuring into something unknown and the kind of apprehension that goes along with ill intent.

"We will only be minutes to the office, Tobias. Follow me, and don't fall behind. I like to walk briskly in the morning," Ebenezer gently commanded.

"Uncle, I know these streets as well as I know the lines in me hand. Let me show you a shorter way," Tobias offered eagerly.

"That is a grand idea, Tobias, but for today let me take you my trusted way. I wouldn't want to be lost learning a new route. Not today. I must be at the prime minister's office directly after leaving you. We can try your way tomorrow, all right?"

"A meeting with the prime minister? The Prime Minister of England?" Tobias asked with untamed curiosity.

"The very one. I have a matter to broach with him that cannot wait. He has a brief window of time when he can see me before he is in session this morning, so we must not dawdle. Once I have introduced you to the office staff and seen to it you are settled in, I will have to be on my way."

Ebenezer led Tobias at a quick pace. He had no time to lose this morning, yet he wanted to assure that Tobias was welcomed well at his office and made to feel comfortable before leaving. He had made arrangements with the prime minister's secretary to meet with him. It had been a difficult task to find time that suited the prime minister's schedule, but Ebenezer had been most accommodating to secure the meeting. He was anxious to discuss the issue of child labour and the steps that could be taken to legislate the ban of its use in industry.

It was only moments before they were at the door of Ebenezer's office. Ebenezer led Tobias into the building through the main door that faced the street. This had been the only entrance used since he acquired the building with Jacob over twenty years ago. Bob was already in his office preparing for the work orders of the day. Outside his office stood the clerk's desk, which Bob's son Peter used to do his work. Beside Peter was an identical desk that stood empty. This would be Tobias' desk. It had been cleared and cleaned in anticipation of his arrival.

"A very good morning to you, Bob and Master Peter," Ebenezer said as he entered the office.

"And to you, Ebenezer." Bob had finally gotten used to addressing Ebenezer by his first name.

"I see you have someone with you today. Is this Tobias, our new assistant clerk?" Bob asked with a smile.

"None other! Now Bob, I want you to make Tobias feel welcome and settled by the time I return. I must go straightaway. I have a very important meeting to attend to. I should be back by noon," Ebenezer replied as he dashed out the door.

Ebenezer was running late and didn't want to chance delaying his arrival, so he decided to hail a coach to take him to the prime minister's office. By chance he spotted a coach turning the corner onto his street. He quickly raised his hand to catch the attention of the driver, and the coach and its team of horses came to a sliding stop just feet from the spot Ebenezer stood waiting.

"I need to get to 10 Downing Street as quickly as your horses can muster. One never keeps the prime minister waiting," Ebenezer remarked to the coach driver as he climbed into the passenger seat. The coach driver snapped his whip, and the horses were off with a jolt. Ebenezer, now at ease, sat back, knowing that he would not be late for his important meeting.

Chapter 7

A Visit with the Prime Minister

The ride to 10 Downing Street seemed to take no time at all. The coach stopped directly in front of the imposing door that had the number ten cast in polished brass and displayed prominently on its door frame. Ebenezer paid the driver with a generous tip and stepped down onto the cobblestone walk that led up to the entrance. The garden surrounding it was neatly manicured. There was no plant or blade of grass that was out of place. It had been maintained this way since the building was used as the office of the prime minister as far back as 1756. Now not only was it his and his staff's offices, but his official residence as well. Ebenezer appreciated the pristine appearance and the work that went into maintaining it; however, he could not help but think at what cost it had come to the taxpayer and whether the money used to maintain this impressive building would have been better spent feeding the poor or housing those without work.

As Ebenezer approached the front door to knock, it was opened by a butler dressed in a black buttoned waist coat and tails. He wore white gloves and black shoes that were so polished Ebenezer could see his reflection in them.

"You must be Mr. Scrooge?" asked the butler as he motioned for Ebenezer to follow him into a waiting room.

"Yes, I have a nine o'clock meeting with his lordship," Ebenezer responded as he looked around the room he was led into.

It was a small room with bookshelves from floor to ceiling on each of the four walls. There was what seemed like a hole cut out of the bookshelf on the right side of the room, and tucked into it was a window ledge and padded bench. On the bench was a book with its pages left open to an illustrated page showing a picture of a black slave in shackles on the deck of a ship. There was a white man with a whip in his hand poised to strike the black man on his back. Ebenezer had known of the slave trade and the pain it had caused countless native Africans throughout the past two centuries. It had made many Englishmen rich, and he himself had been tempted to take advantage of what was viewed as a lucrative business opportunity. But he had decided not to diversify his business holdings for some reason. Perhaps it was because he had always traded in hard tangibles like property and commodities. Or maybe it was because he had a business sense that this kind of trade would eventually be put to an end and investment in it was too high a risk. Whatever the reason, it was not for humanitarian causes that he had refrained from investing in the slave trade. His decisions had always been cold and calculating, without any consideration for humanity. His business sense, however, was quite accurate. For it was recently, under the government of Lord Grey, that the slave abolition statutes had begun to shift. It was, in fact, under the prime minister's leadership that these brutal practices had finally been tabled in Parliament and were, for the first time since slavery began, being addressed.

Lord Grey had shown himself to be a man of conviction and compassion. Knowing this, Ebenezer was hopeful that he would have a sympathetic ear, and a powerful ally in lobbying for the abolition of a new kind of forced labour that of Britain's children.

"Why, Ebenezer Scrooge, it is always good to see you, my old friend!" exclaimed the prime minister as he entered the room with the grace and poise of a well-bred British aristocrat.

"And always a pleasure to see you, James, whether it be personal or business," replied Ebenezer.

"So then, what is your pleasure today, personal or business?" asked the prime minister.

"It is both personal and business, I'm afraid."

"Well then, I think we should take some time on this over a strong cup of our tea. Shall I ring for tea service?" asked the prime minister as he pulled a satin cord that hung from an opening in the ceiling.

Before he had sat down the butler who had greeted Ebenezer at the front door appeared.

"You rang, sir?" responded the butler, anticipating any request the prime minister would ask of him.

"Yes, Simmons, could you fetch a pot of strong Grey for us? We may be a while, so please inform my secretary that my next appointment will be delayed," requested the prime minister.

"Now then, Ebenezer, you have my complete attention for as long as you need me this morning."

"I know your time is too valuable to waste, so I will get right down to it. There is a humanitarian crisis that is as insidious as the African slave trade and is never spoken about."

"Go on. I am listening. I know a great deal about this slave trade issue. It has consumed my ministers in cabinet since I took office."

"I must commend you. I know that you have worked hard this past year to bring the dialogue of the abolition of slavery to the forefront. To have it finally tabled in Parliament must be, for you, a great accomplishment."

"It has been worth every bit of the struggle, fight, and conflict it took to achieve our desired end thus far."

"Is there enough of that fight still in you to go another round?"

"If the cause is as worthy as the last, I have the rest of my political lifetime to give to it."

"This is a cause as worthy, if not more so. For it concerns our own born here, on home soil. I have been a witness to it myself for years but am only now seeing the catastrophic effects it is levying on a whole generation. James, I implore you to hear what I know to be true. As we speak there are thousands of children across England not in school as they should be but in factories and mines working in indecent conditions with very long hours and pennies for pay," explained Ebenezer as the prime minister looked on intently.

"I know that there are some who are not fit for schooling or cannot afford the basics in clothing and books to attend. These few are attended to and provided for through the work they perform. In fact, there was a report of this very subject tabled in the house just a fortnight ago. The findings revealed that the working conditions were compliant with those of the standards set for all factories and mines and that when room and boarding were considered, compensation was rated to be fair," interjected the prime minister with the tone and confidence of a seasoned parliamentarian.

"This report is wrong, or at best misleading, James. I know; I have seen it with my own eyes. The housing is crowded and filthy. The board consists of a piece of barely buttered bread and broth three times a day. Slaves are fed better than most of these children who work fourteen hour days, day after day, without rest, school, or play. I will take you to see it for yourself right here in London. And there are thousands more throughout the country, all with workforces younger than you would believe, James," replied Ebenezer with mounting emotion.

"I trust your word, my friend. But for me to have a chance of convincing Parliament to even consider this issue, I need more than your conviction."

"Then proof you shall have. I will take you to several such work mills and then have you back to my home to meet my housekeeper's children. They will tell you their stories that will give you all the convincing evidence you will need."

"I have never seen you with such fervor. You would make a convincing political leader, Ebenezer. I would always have a place for someone of your dedication in my cabinet. Have you ever considered politics as a way to effect change?"

"I am a man of business, James. I leave the politics of persuasion to men like you. That is the reason I came to see you this morning. You have made a name for yourself in moving the collective will of the people to your way of thinking. In only one term you have managed to begin the change in legislation concerning slave ownership and the process to end slavery in the entire British Empire. This has been no small feat and one that does not come about by chance. James, I ask you to now use that same acuity to effect change in the child labour laws that are destroying an entire generation."

"Take me to see what you have seen. If it is as you say it is, you have my word that I will move this forward in Parliament."

Ebenezer felt at that moment there was a significant shift about to take place in the condition of humanity, a shift that would begin a process of change, leading to the betterment for those most helpless. He remembered what Jacob had told him of seeing all the suffering in the world but lacking the power to do anything about it. Ebenezer realized now exactly what Jacob was trying to tell him. He knew now that he had both the ability and the power to make a difference in his world, a difference that would last for generations. As the prime minister led Ebenezer to the front entrance, they discussed the details for their surprise factory visits. Neither of them noticed a link of twelve chains appear on the seat of the chair that the prime minister had occupied during their conversation. Ebenezer's feelings were, indeed, correct. He had just influenced the initiation of change that would bring redemption to a lost generation.

Chapter 8

The Temptation

It turned out that Peter was an excellent working companion for Tobias. He withheld no detail Tobias required to do his duties as an assistant clerk. Peter showed him how to enter payments into the ledger book and how to balance the journals for the end of the day. Tobias was a quick learner, only having to be shown something once before he understood it. Most coworkers would have reacted with jealousy and mistrust, but Peter acted quite differently. He had taken a liking to Tobias and saw his being in the office as a welcomed change and chance to talk to someone closer to his own age. Tobias was fortunate to have the chance to work with someone who was so supportive and genuinely interested in helping him. For his first job in an office with structure and work standards he could not have found a better match. His desk sat adjacent to Peter's, with only an arm's length between them. There could be nothing unnoticed by the other.

"And how much have you learned today, Tobias? Are you running my business yet?" chuckled Ebenezer, as he entered the office after returning from his visit with the prime minister.

"Master Peter tells me I'm a very quick learner. I've already learned how to receipt and deposit rent payments," replied Tobias with a visible sign of pride.

"Well then, it won't be long before you are in charge. I'm pleased to see that you have fit in, and so quickly, Tobias," replied Ebenezer with a pondering look in his eye. He was thinking about Tobias' mother and the promise that he had made to arrange better care for her in a private facility. He didn't want Tobias to know what he was planning quite yet, so he fabricated an excuse for having to leave the office once again.

"My, where is my mind today! I completely forgot the appointment I have with my solicitor. I shall not be back this afternoon, and with Bob away spending time with Tiny Tim, you two are in charge for the rest of the day. Peter, since it is Tobias' first day on the job, you'd best be the one to close the office when the day is done. Right then, I'm off. Oh, one more thing I nearly forgot—I am having a grand party to celebrate the arrival of Tobias to the household. The day after tomorrow we finish work at five o'clock so that we can begin the festivities without delay! Don't forget to tell your father, Peter. And make sure your mother and your brothers and sisters know that they too are invited." With that, Ebenezer was on his way.

He did not like to mislead them by saying he was going to see his solicitor when his intention was to seek out the public hospital where Tobias' mother was. He then got the notion to pay a visit to his solicitor, not just to satisfy his conscience for having lied, but to actually conduct business with him. Ebenezer had wanted to discuss the legalities of becoming Tobias' guardian, and this seemed like as good a time as any to start the process. He took the chance that his solicitor would be engaged with other clients, but he figured that he would not have to wait long to meet without an appointment; Ebenezer was his solicitor's top client and had privileges that only he was afforded. He redirected his steps toward Fenchurch Street, to the offices of Mr. Gerald Striker, solicitor and public notary. Mr. Striker had been Ebenezer's solicitor since he began in business. He had overseen hundreds of Ebenezer's business transactions over the years. Most were of dubious nature, but today's business was different, as different as Ebenezer had become himself. He now wanted to become a cornerstone influence for Tobias. Tobias did not have a father figure in his life, and as a result he had strayed from the care and concern of a loving mother to satisfy the innate need for male acceptance from those who would pay him the slightest attention. The only ones who did were the shysters and scammers that are found in any city the size of London. It was not his doing that led him into a life of thievery. For without a strong fatherly influence, Tobias was bound to fall from society's grace. Ebenezer had decided that he would be that fatherly influence Tobias needed to have in order to have any chance of changing his errant ways. As Ebenezer stood in his solicitor's office to discuss the process, he wondered what Tobias would think if he knew about what was soon to happen.

Tobias had only one thing on his mind, and that was how he was going to get his mother out of that defiled hospital. As he sat at his desk beside Peter, he began to calculate ways he could extract the needed monies from Ebenezer's business. He knew that he would have the opportunity to handle rent money that was brought in by the tenants of Ebenezer's vast lot of rental houses throughout London. He decided that, given the chance, he would collect the funds, and instead of receiving them into the ledger as he had been instructed to do, he would pocket them and make no record of the transaction. If there was no one else in the office to witness the collection of the rent monies, then he would get away with it undetected until much later in the year when a full audit of the accounts would be conducted. By then, he would be long gone and would have his mother out of the hospital. All he had to do was wait for the opportunity to be alone in the office when a tenant came to pay their rent.

"It is colder than the Highlands in here," shouted Peter as he checked the coal stove in the back corner of the general office. As he opened the door to the stove, he noticed a dwindling pile of coal ambers about to die out.

"No wonder, then. There's hardly one glowing ember of coal left!" Peter glanced at the coal buckets beside the stove, finding them empty.

"If we want to stay warm, we'll need more coal. The coal merchant is over on Leadenhall Street. I'll go there and get a slew of coal before he closes for the day. You'll be fine here by yourself till I get back?" asked Peter as he put on his coat and cap.

"I can handle things. I have a teacher who has taught me well. I'll be fine. Just go before we both freeze solid to our desks!" exclaimed Tobias with a pondering glance.

Could this be the chance opportunity he was hoping for? He began desperately churning in his mind how he could execute a quick plan. All he needed was for a client to come to the office and transact a payment. However, the chance of that happening before Peter returned was most unlikely. As he stared out the window onto the street, an idea came to him. What if, instead, he went to the client rather than the client coming to him? He remembered Peter saying to him earlier in the day that there was a tenant whose rent was due today and that he expected them to be in to settle up. But who were they, and where did they live? Perhaps Peter had recorded their name on one of the scattered papers on his desk. He began to quickly sort through each one looking for a name or address that might be the client's he was looking for. He found nothing that appeared to be the name. When he reached the last sheet on the pile, he had all but given up. He almost missed what he was searching for, and if it wasn't for the odd angle and the style of the letters written on the page, he most surely would have. The note read "Moore, due today—fifteen shillings and six pence." He had now remembered and knew that this was the name Peter had mentioned. All he had to do was find the correct address and he would be on his way to collect. He had been shown earlier in the day a large filing cupboard that housed a file on each client in Ebenezer's business. He walked across the room to it and opened wide the large wooden doors to reveal a wall of minutely labeled files all ordered by name. The *M*s were halfway down on the second shelf. He fingered file by file until he came to Moore. The file contained single sheets mixed with scribbled notes. All he needed was the address for the Moores, and without any trouble he found it neatly written on the top of the third sheet in. It read, "Moore, Richard—589 Pudding Lane." This was only five minutes by foot from the office. If he hurried, he could be there and back before Peter returned with the stove coal buckets.

Quickly grabbing his jacket hanging on a hook behind the office door, Tobias was on his way to complete his task. He knew these streets and had used this knowledge many times to dodge the pursuit of the law. Like a fox slipping in and out of the shadows, Tobias arrived at his destination without being noticed. The door he was about to knock on appeared weathered and in need of a fresh coat of paint. The maintenance of the tenant houses was marginal at the best of times. The tenants seldom did anything themselves to improve their surroundings, so most maintenance fell to the landlord. He knocked strongly three times and waited to hear movement from behind the door. The tenant could be in the home but avoiding answering the door for fear it was Ebenezer or one of his clerks come to collect the rent. The advantage Tobias had this day was he was not yet known by any of the tenants, so he would not be taken for a rent collector. He knocked again, this time with more resolve. He knew this was his only chance of obtaining the money he needed, and this gave him the determination to stay the course. On the third knock the door opened, and a tall man only half dressed appeared at the entrance. Clinging to his leg was a young boy about three years old.

"Can I help you?" asked the man.

"My name is Tobias Harding, and I'm in the employ of Mr. Scrooge. I understand you have a rent due today, and I have come to collect it for you and save you having to come to our office," replied Tobias with a strong confident voice.

"Why that is good of you, young man. I have it ready in an envelope in my bedchamber. Would you step in while I go get it for you?" asked the man as he gestured for Tobias to enter.

Tobias stood in the front entrance of the man's home waiting for him to return. He could not help but notice the emptiness of the house. In the front parlor where there would usually be sofas and side tables stood just one lonely wooden chair with a small three-legged stool beside it. On the stool was a single candlestick melted down nearly to its base. The melted wax had formed a solid pool covering the seat. At the end of the hallway was the kitchen that looked as empty as the parlour. A wood stove stood with its door open. There was no sign of a fire or any wood to start one. In the corner was a small table with no chairs. Tobias wondered if this man and his family was planning to move and had packed away their possessions, or was it that they could simply not afford to properly furnish their home.

"Here it is, the full amount. You can count it if you like," offered the man as he came down the stairs with the rent envelope in his hand.

"That won't be necessary, Mr. Moore. I trust it is all here. On behalf of Mr. Scrooge, I thank you for keeping your payments current."

As Tobias said this, he was overcome with a feeling of guilt he had never felt before. The streets had hardened his heart, and guilt was not an emotion he was accustomed to struggle with. He was going to use these funds that belonged to Mr. Scrooge and use them for his own purposes. He had rationalized a hundred times that the use of these wrongly acquired monies was for a noble end. He did not welcome these feelings, fearing they would weaken his resolve. He tried to erase them from his thoughts. As he walked out the door to make his way back to the counting house, he could not shake them from his mind. A change of conscience had begun to take seed in him. He would soon begin to sense the real difference between right and wrong. It was a change he eventually could not resist; a change begun by what Ebenezer had done for him. It was a change, however, that was about to be tested.

As he turned the corner onto Wigmore Street, he saw a far-too-familiar face approaching him. It was Tagger. Word travels fast through the underbelly of London, and Tagger had come to seek what fortune he could suck from Tobias' newly acquired position. Tagger had been his partner in many of his scheming thieveries. They had known each other for many years and had experienced many narrow escapes together. They had been very close, like brothers, but Tobias knew that if he was to leave that world behind he would have to leave Tagger there as well. He was about to find out that it would not be that easy to do so.

"So I hears you 'ave moved up in the world, Mr. Harding?" sneered Tagger as he took notice of Tobias' new clothes. "Oh, aren't we a fancy gentlemen. How does it feel to be on the other side of the street now, me friend?"

"You are no friend of mine anymore, Tagger. I've started a new life, and I'm letting go of my past."

"Letting go of our past, are we? Isn't that good for the soul now? Well, you'd better remember some of us who helped you along the way, Mr. Fancy Dress. You owe me for the times I saved your skin from landing back in jail."

"You didn't help this last time, now did you?"

"No, that's true. I did hear, though, that Mr. Ebenezer Scrooge was the sod who got you out. Isn't that right, huh?"

"What if it was?"

"I understand that this Mr. Scrooge is quite well-to-do and that you are living at his well-to-do address."

"And what if I was? Why would you care?"

"Oh, I care, me friend. I really care. Especially when you are going to help me find a way into this Mr. Scrooge's house and get me some of his things he ain't going to miss."

"And what makes you think I'm going to help you with that?"

"Your mom still in that hospital, is she? Still looking for a way to get her out of there, I bet?"

"I don't need you for that. I have my own plan."

"Well, if you are anything like you was, you have more than one plan. Plans don't always work out. You should always have another in your back pocket. Isn't that what you taught me?"

Tagger was right. He had always made plans with at least one in reserve, just in case the first one didn't work. Tobias found himself beginning to think again the way he did back on the street.

"You're right. I always did have a second plan. So what do you have in mind?"

Chapter 9

The Guardianship

"Are you sure this is what you want to do, Ebenezer? Taking on the responsibility of this young impudent lad will not be without its challenges," questioned Mr. Striker.

"I am fully aware of my potential responsibilities, Gerald. If no one is willing to build into the lives of others, then this world will remain a cold and self-centered place filled with individuals measuring their fortune in life with only their position and possessions without any notion of concern for those less fortunate than themselves," replied Ebenezer, hoping to impact the thinking of his longtime solicitor and friend.

"You are quite right, if not a little altruistic. I do applaud you for doing what you have decided to do. I must admit, though, that it is taking some getting used to knowing you in this new way. It is inspiring to see that such a self-possessed man as you were is now such a bright beacon of social betterment," exclaimed Mr. Striker.

"I would only take such a contrived compliment like that from you, Gerald," replied Ebenezer thinking he was beginning to have some influence on his friend's thinking. That gave him great pleasure.

"I must be on my way; there is no time to waste today. My next duty is to pay a visit to Tobias' mother, who lays suffering in a public infirmary. I need her blessing on my plan before I can move forward on this. Thank you, Gerald, for your professional acumen in this matter. I trust this will all remain confidential until my choosing?" asked Ebenezer as he put on his coat and hat.

"My lips are as tight as a monk sworn to silence," replied Mr. Striker.

"I know I can always count on your discretion, Gerald. Oh, I almost forgot—please stop by the house after your work is done the day after next. I have planned a party to celebrate Tobias's arrival."

"It would be my pleasure to join in the festivities. I will close the office early to make sure I don't miss out on Mrs. Nottingham's roast beef. She is planning to serve it?" Mr. Striker asked with anticipation.

"I will go to the butcher myself to purchase one if need be!" replied Ebenezer as he left en route to Charing Cross Hospital.

Chapter 10

Fishing the Thames

The infirmary was in the west end of London, not quite close enough to go to on foot. He would have to find a carriage for hire. There was a carriage station on Belvedere Road, two streets south of the Thames. It would require a crossing over the Waterloo Bridge only to return back, but he knew there was always a horse and carriage waiting there for the next paying passenger. He made the only reasonable decision and began his trek southward.

Ebenezer had travelled these streets many times before; in the past it was to visit his tenants and collect rents due or to evict the delinquent ones. Ebenezer no longer evicted anyone. If someone was past due on their rent, he would work with them to help restore their affairs. Often it was due to the loss of work, in which case he would help them find new employment. Other times there were unexpected expenses that crippled a household. Ebenezer would cover the bills and make sure they were not being exploited or cheated. For as many enemies as he had before, he was now a friend to tenfold more. As he crossed the river, he noticed a small dory with a lone fisherman tending to his catch. As the fisherman pulled it in, he could see what seemed to be a handsome bounty of fish flapping and tossing about.

"Is your fish for sale?" shouted Ebenezer from the top of the bridge.

"Are you fancying fish for dinner tonight, then?" asked the fisherman.

Ebenezer did, in fact, enjoy a fish meal, and had Mrs. Nottingham prepare it for him at least once a week. He would have her purchase the fish from the fishmongers at Covent Gardens market, but the idea of a fresh catch directly from the river prompted his impulsive response.

"Why, yes I would. In fact, I'll take your entire catch. How much can I give you for it?"

"Me whole catch? Who might you be looking for the whole lot? I only deal with the mongers at Covent Garden. I'm not interested in selling to nobody else." replied the fisherman.

"I don't want you to get any less than you would at the market, my good man, and I am certainly not looking to thwart any of your trading arrangements."

"Then explain to me why you want to take me whole catch then?" asked the fisherman skeptically.

"The fish will do a great deal of good for a great deal of needful people." replied Ebenezer in earnest.

"What are you then, some kind of saint?" sneered the fisherman.

"No sir, I am not a saint, just someone wanting to do some good in a world that needs a little mercy."

"Well, I suppose I shouldn't care what you want to do with the catch, just as long as I get me market price."

"I'll give you the highest price you have ever been offered, and I'll pay you in pound sterling. The only thing I ask is that you deliver all of it to Charing Cross Hospital. Do you know where that is?" asked Ebenezer.

"I do. It is up on Agar Street. I had me young lad in there not too long back with a broken leg. They took good care of him, they did. But there was plenty who were quite sick and looked like they'd been laid up for quite a spell." replied the fisherman.

"Most go there to die. I'm on my way there now to help at least one of those poor souls escape that fate. So what do you say—can we do a good deed together?"

"I suppose I can't refuse, since it's going to do such good? The most I have ever fetched for a catch this size was five pounds, ten shillings."

"How about I give you ten pounds, then?"

"Ten pounds? You can't be serious? Who did you say you was?"

"I do not believe I have introduced myself. Ebenezer Scrooge is my name, and I can assure you, sir that I am good for the sum offered to you."

"Scrooge, Ebenezer Scrooge? Why, everyone knows you as a nasty, niggardly old man who would never do nothing for anyone else, and you're telling me you want to give me catch to all the dying patients at Charing Cross? I'm not convinced."

"I am, my good man. But I am not who I was. I stand here as proof that the human heart can change and begin to seek the welfare of others above its own."

"Show me the ten pounds then, and I might be inclined to believe you." demanded the fisherman. Ebenezer took his billfold from his coat pocket, and began to count out the pound notes. He held the money up and waved it at the fisherman.

"Ten pounds as offered." announced Ebenezer hanging on to the guard rail of the bridge.

"It's a pleasure to meet you, Mr. Scrooge. I believe we have ourselves a deal." replied the fisherman, convinced that Ebenezer was who he claimed to be.

"Say, would you be planning to take those fish directly to the infirmary?" asked Ebenezer, hoping to get a ride, and save the nuisance of finding a carriage for hire.

"Straightaway. I have a delivery wagon that has room for two, if that's what you're thinking. I can take you with me if you don't mind a rough ride. It's not the fine carriage a man of your station is accustomed to, but you'll get there sooner than waiting for a hired coach."

"It would be my pleasure to accompany you. You know, we have been talking and you now know who I am, but I have not gotten your name. To whom do I have the pleasure of speaking?" asked Ebenezer as he tipped his hat with a gesture of respect toward the fisherman.

"My name is Richard Gordon. I am the third generation of Gordons to fish the Thames. It hasn't made any of us rich, but I wouldn't want to do anything else."

"It is an honest and worthy vocation, Mr. Gordon. You are a fortunate man that you can make your way in this world and be content with your position in it. That may be the best definition of happiness a man could ever want."

"Well, I can honestly say I am quite content, not knowing any other way. So perhaps I am happy. How about you, Mr. Scrooge? What makes you happy?"

"For me, there is no greater delight than to see someone's life changed and their dignity restored. Each one of us deserves the respect, and genuine concern from others. When I can help to make that happen, I am truly fulfilled."

"If everyone thought like you, the world would be a much better place. You certainly make a man think, Mr. Scrooge."

"Perhaps not everyone thinks as I do, but if we each impacted the thinking of just one other, then we would be well on our way to this better world. Now, we'd best be getting to the infirmary with the catch. I'll come down to the riverbank to where you are. I take it your wagon is not far from the shore?"

"By the time you are down from the bridge, Mr. Scrooge I will have the full lot of fish in the back and the horses harnessed and waiting." replied Mr. Gordon.

Ebenezer began his descent down the set of wrought iron stairs located along side of the bridge. Neither of them heard the sound, or noticed the chain link that dropped from out of the sky above the bridge where they stood talking.

Chapter 11

The Flower Lady

Ebenezer made his way toward Mr. Gordon's wagon. The horses were already hitched up, and Mr. Gordon was loading the fish onto the cart bed. He didn't even notice the stark, inescapable smell of fish. Nor did he see the thick coat of scales that covered the wagon from years of constant use. Ebenezer was no longer too proud to be with others of a lower social standing. He was able to look beyond the visible and seek the modesty that comes with the humbling of the heart.

"I do appreciate you taking me along with you. I have never seen London from the perch of a fisherman's wagon, and I do believe I will enjoy the change from the encasement of a covered coach," commented Ebenezer as he stepped up on the wagon and sat down on the passenger side of the bench seat.

"It is an honour to have you as my passenger, Mr. Scrooge," replied Mr. Gordon as he climbed up himself and sat in the driver seat.

"My lips won't rest until I've told all who I know in London that I've met the most generous man in this city, and his name is Ebenezer Scrooge."

He picked up the reins and gave a quick whip motion to the horses, signaling them to move. Without a hair's delay the duo of Clydesdales advanced up a slight embankment to the roadway that ran along the river's edge. The hospital was not a great distance from where they were; it would only take them minutes to arrive at the pace the horses were moving.

"I do appreciate what you said to me earlier on the bridge about you wanting to change the way you think about things. I have come to understand that life is mostly about attitude and little about circumstance. With the right attitude, you can help change others," said Ebenezer as he glanced left and right at the streets of London he had seen time and time again; only now it was from a more telling point of view.

This time he noticed the children in the street having great fun playing with a barrel ring and a couple of sticks. They were trying to see who could keep the ring rolling the longest. It reminded him of when he was a young boy and how much fun he had playing with his boyhood friends. It was a time in his life when his heart was light and carefree. Those childhood feelings were beginning to return to him, and it made him feel young again. As they turned the corner and continued toward the hospital, he noticed a flower lady trying to sell her heather sprigs to whoever would buy them. She stood patiently as most passed her by. She looked cold and tired standing alone. Her clothes were worn and inadequate for the winter chill. She had a gentle and kind face that surely had seen many troubles and heartaches. He could not help thinking that he had probably passed her by himself many times over the years and had never once stopped to buy a flower from her.

"Can you stop for one moment please, Mr. Gordon? I need to make a purchase that I should have made long ago," Ebenezer asked as he stepped down from the wagon and made his way toward the woman. She held in her hand several bunches of heather. Although she looked weathered and tired, she still managed to smile at all who passed her by.

"Your flowers are like a handful of comfort on this dreary day, Miss. I will take all that you have with you, and I want to pay you ten times what you normally charge," Ebenezer stated firmly. The woman looked at him as if he were crazy.

"I am not trying to trick you. I truly mean what I say. I want to pay you what I think your flowers are worth to me—all of them. They will bring such joy to someone in need of them; they may even help her to get better. There is no price you can put on that, now can you?" replied Ebenezer, trying to put the woman at ease.

"I'm sorry for reacting that way, sir, but, I ain't never been offered more for me flowers than what I ask, and ten times that, oh my word!" exclaimed the woman, trying to return to her composed state again as they continued to talk.

"I want you to take the extra and buy yourself a warm coat so that you don't freeze to death standing here all day. I also want you to start delivering your flowers to my home weekly. There is nothing as lovely as a vase full of fresh flowers to fill the house with their heavenly scent. Here is my address. You can go there now, if you wish, and speak to my housekeeper, Mrs. Nottingham. Tell her I sent you to make the arrangement for the deliveries." Ebenezer took a piece of writing paper he always kept in his billfold for just this kind of situation. He wrote on the paper "64 Chesterfield Hill." The woman looked at it with noticeable embarrassment. Ebenezer realized that she did not know how to read the note. He quickly responded to avoid embarrassing her any further.

"Oh dear, I do have illegible hand writing, don't I? Please forgive me. My address is sixty-four Chesterfield Hill. Do you know it?"

"Why that ain't too far from heres. I know how to get there. And who mights you be, kind sir? I would like to thank you proper like," she asked.

"I am your humble servant, Ebenezer Scrooge," he replied.

"Not the Ebenezer Scrooge? But he's no one like you. You are too kind and generous to be him. Are you playing with me?" she questioned, not believing him.

"I never lie, and especially not to as fine a young lady as you, Miss —?"

"Emily Rose Sinclair is me name."

"That is a very pretty name, Miss Emily Rose. With a name like that, you were destined to be a purveyor of all things beautiful and fragrant."

"You are kind, and charming too, Mr. Scrooge. You've certainly lightened me day. Life's situation isn't so bad when you see there's good in even the worst of us all."

"Yes, you have got it! You have just hit on the essence of the joy that everyone can have if they only open their eyes to it. Look for the good and you will find it. I look forward to a bouquet of your flowers every week from now on, Miss Emily Rose." Ebenezer tipped his hat to her and returned to the fish wagon.

She turned in the direction of Chesterfield Hill and had only taken two steps when she heard what seemed to be the sound of metal hitting the ground. She turned back and noticed a chain link lying in a crack of two cobblestones in the street. She thought it was strange and wondered where it could have fallen from. Looking up all she saw was clear sky.

Chapter 12

An Unexpected Encounter

"This is it, Mr. Scrooge, Charing Cross Hospital. Did you want me to drop you off here at the front while I take the stock of fish through the service alley?" asked Mr. Gordon as they drew up to the main entrance. It was a stately-looking building with tall marble columns framing the large double oak front doors. Over the years it had become known as a place of last resort. Most came there to suffer their last days.

"Why don't I go in to talk to the staff in charge and arrange for the delivery of the fish out back," suggested Ebenezer, climbing down off the wagon.

"That makes sense to me. I'm sure there will be someone in the back to receive the goods," replied Mr. Gordon.

As he directed the horses down the back alley of the hospital, Ebenezer climbed the stairs leading to the imposing front entrance. With some effort he opened the heavy doors and made his way through the foyer to what seemed like an administrator's station. Seated behind a desk was a man in his late fifties wearing a white medical coat over a stiffly starched collared shirt with a dull patterned necktie. He was preoccupied with filling out what were, most likely, patient records.

"Can I help you? Are you here to see a patient or to speak to a member of our staff?" asked the man, raising his eyes over the rim of his glasses. He continued to sit at the desk, not bothering to get out of his seat to greet Ebenezer.

"Both, actually. I came to visit Mrs. Harding. Before I do that, however, I would like to make arrangements for the delivery of a stock of freshly caught fish. The fisherman's wagon is at your delivery door right now," smiled Ebenezer, anxious to share the news of his gift to the hospital.

"I don't believe we have fish on order. Perhaps you have the wrong hospital. Are you sure it is for Charing Cross?" asked the man as he began flipping through a stack of outstanding orders that were in a file on the corner of his desk.

"Oh, you won't find an order for this fish delivery in that file. The fish are a gift to the patients and staff. They were caught in the Thames this very morning. Any fresher and they would jump out of the wagon themselves!" laughed Ebenezer.

"Oh, well then. We can't take an unsolicited order of fish from just anyone. There are policies that govern these situations," replied the administrator sternly.

"How about compassion and concern? Where do they factor into your hospital's policies?"

"I am not certain what you mean, Mr. . . . . . ?"

"The name is Scrooge, Ebenezer Scrooge."

"Oh, I am sorry Mr. Scrooge, sir. I did not know that this was your gift. By all means we can most certainly accept it knowing who it comes from."

"And what if it didn't come from me but from another well-meaning citizen? Would you have rejected this gift that could give nourishment and health to those who are sick if it had?"

"Well, Mr. Scrooge, the point is that we are in possession of your generous donation now, and we will make good use of it to provide additional nourishment to the patients," replied the administrator, trying to redirect the conversation.

"In the future, I would suggest that you revise your policies and procedures to accommodate any well-intended gift to the hospital. Now that we have that taken care of, may I ask in which ward Mrs. Doris Harding would be?" asked Ebenezer. The administrator paged through a patient file until he came to Mrs. Harding.

"Oh yes, Mrs. Harding; she is in the south ward. You go straight down this hall, through the double doors, and then turn to your right. Follow the signs for the south ward, and if you get disorientated, any of the staff can direct you," replied the administrator in a pleasant and accommodating tone. He was much better at dealing with hospital guests, it seemed, than he was with donor relations Ebenezer thought as he made his way to the ward where Mrs. Harding would be found.

The hallways felt stark and sterile. There was no colour on the walls, no pictures or texture of any kind. Ebenezer found it rather depressing. He reminded himself that he was in an institutional facility where function, not form, was the only concern. He wound his way through the narrow halls, watching for the signs that would lead him to the south ward. As he was turning a corner he came upon a nursing station, vacant of any staff. They must all be attending to their patients in the ward, he thought. Just as he was going to open a door that led to the south ward, an elderly nurse appeared carrying a glass vial and a gauze roll.

"Can I help you, sir? You look far too healthy to be a patient. Who might you be here to visit?" asked the nurse in an officious voice.

"Oh, you are quite right about me not being a patient; I am here to see Mrs. Doris Harding. Can you direct me to her bedside?" replied Ebenezer, hoping he had arrived at the right place.

"Mrs. Harding is convalescing in bed thirty-two. She is just receiving her meal from Nurse Pearce. You may have to wait until they are finished, but go ahead in. Are you a friend or family member?"

"I am a friend whom she is about to meet for the first time," replied Ebenezer. The nurse looked slightly puzzled by his remark but paid little attention to it as she continued on with her duties.

He entered through the double glass doors that stood several yards from the nursing station. He could not ignore the nagging thought on his mind as he walked down the centre aisle of the ward looking for number thirty-two. The name Pearce had a familiarity to it, but he could not place it. He began going through the names and places of the encounters he had had both present and past, but it was not coming to him. Just then, he noticed that he had passed number thirty-one. Doris Harding was in the next bed. He walked up behind a woman wearing a nurse's uniform sitting with her back to him. He could see the face of the woman lying in the bed. She was quite old and sickly looking. She wore a wool head scarf and had a well-worn shawl draped over her shoulders. The nurse was hand-feeding her a clear broth that was steaming up from the bowl. She turned as she heard Ebenezer approach, revealing her face to him. She was a beautiful older woman with fine features. Her hair was silky and dark with accents of white made up and covered by her nursing cap. Her face was like an angel's that glowed with a gentle spirit. Her warm brown eyes seemed familiar to him. When her eyes met his he knew from where this familiarity had come. He felt a rush of intense emotion rise up. It was the emotion experienced in his tender youth when he was struck by the first allure of romance. It had been a time of impulse and intrigue; it was a time of total abandonment of reason. It was a time when he had felt truly in love. Sitting before him was the only woman he had ever given his heart to. She was the woman he was to wed; she was the woman he was to start a family with, and grow old with. The woman seated before him was Belle Pearce. He knew her from when he was a young apprentice so many years before. It was at the Christmas party held at the offices of Mr. Fezziwig where they first met. He could remember when he first laid eyes on her that evening and how he was drawn to her instantly. They talked and danced the whole night, and when the party came to an end he requested to meet her the next day. It turned into a romance that soon led to an engagement. Those were the happiest days of his life, but they had long since been buried deep in his sub-conscience and erased from his heart. He would not feel love like hers again. It had been over forty years since the day she released him from his bond of engagement. She said that she could not be with a man who put the love of money before her. His efforts to convince her that he could change, that he would change, were unsuccessful. In the end his words rang hollow. Any action he could have taken to win Belle back faded away into darkness, and forged a heart that had become as hard as bedrock. Belle had never seen Ebenezer again after their final words. He never attempted to prove to her that his words were more than thin attempts to convince her of his intentions. Only sincere action, not words, would have made a difference, but he never came back to her, not once. She hoped that he would return and prove to her that his words were spoken with true intent, but the knock on her door was never heard, nor was a letter of regret ever received. He took a step closer to her and, with some reluctance, spoke.

"You must be Nurse Pearce?"

"Yes, I am, and you are?" Ebenezer hesitated to reveal to her who he was. Belle deserved to know who she was speaking with, but he feared her rejection once again.

"I am in charge of Mrs. Harding's son, Tobias. I have come to see if we can find her better care," replied Ebenezer, realizing that what he just said may have offended Belle. "Oh, I do not mean by that she is receiving poor care. On the contrary, I am certain that the care you are giving her is of the highest standard."

"Please, there is no need to explain. It is a well-known fact that Charing Cross is where the sick and poor of London must come. It is for that reason that I chose to be here."

Ebenezer realized that she had not changed in all the years that had passed. She was still the same caring soul who was always concerned more for others than she was for herself. She was still the same woman he had fallen in love with. He found himself beginning to feel the same way he did when they first met. Every part of his body tingled; his head became as light as the morning air.

"There is no doubt that she is receiving the best of care with you by her side," Ebenezer remarked, trying to pull himself back into the present moment.

"I give her the care I can. There are many patients to attend to, and sometimes they only get what we can give."

"I can see that the hospital could do with more staff. Perhaps a word to the chief administrator would help to change things?" replied Ebenezer, already having decided to speak to those in charge.

"I don't know if that would help. We must do with the funds allotted to us; there is no more to pay for new nurses. If you don't mind, I will leave you for a moment. I need to attend to my patients; I will be back soon."

As Belle turned away, Ebenezer approached Mrs. Harding as she lay in her bed with her eyes closed. When he said her name she opened them and looked up and smiled.

"Mrs. Harding, my name is Ebenezer Scrooge. You do not know me, but I have recently taken your son in to live with me."

"Is Tobias in trouble? Is he all right?"

"He is well taken care of and has all that he needs. He got himself in trouble with the law and was in jail for a spell."

"Oh dear, was he caught stealing again?"

"Yes, Mrs. Harding, he was. In fact, he was caught stealing from me."

"He stole from you, and you have him staying in your home? I don't understand."

"If the court would have had its way, Tobias would still be in jail now. I took pity on him and asked the judge to let him come home with me. I want to help your son, Mrs. Harding. He is not a bad lad; he has not been given the chance that others have. That is all."

"Do you really believe that, Mr. Scrooge? I've been so worried about my son. Ever since his father died, Tobias has been a lost soul."

"My dear Mrs. Harding, your son is now under my employment as a junior clerk. He was in trouble with the courts and was about to be put in prison, but I convinced the judge to release Tobias. Your son is a good young man, Mrs. Harding. His intentions are pure. He only wanted to raise enough funds to provide better care for you. He loves you dearly and would do anything to see you well and on your feet again," said Ebenezer, turning to look at Belle, who was returning from attending to another patient. Ebenezer took Belle aside to ask her something that he had just thought of that moment.

"I would like to propose something to you, Nurse Pearce. Can we speak in private?" asked Ebenezer with resolve in his eyes.

"Yes, of course, but is it necessary to leave the ward? Can you not speak openly, or is it a matter of discretion?"

"I don't mean to alarm you, but it is a matter of life or death. It concerns the well-being of Mrs. Harding."

Chapter 13

The Confession

Peter struggled with the two full buckets of stove coal while juggling to open the office door. He called out for Tobias but got no reply; he was in the counting house alone. He took the buckets to the stove room and filled it to capacity. He then took the bellows and fanned the remaining coals until they fired up the new supply. As he was finishing his task the office door opened and a man in his early thirties entered.

"Good day to you, sir. May I be of assistance to you?" asked Peter, wiping the black coal dust from his hands.

"Yes, I believe you can. I just received a visit from one of the other clerks in your office who came to collect my rent. He was very courteous and accommodating, but he forgot to give me a written receipt for my payment. I came by to take care of that. As I was on the way to the butcher, I thought I would drop in on my way."

"I am sorry for your inconvenience. You must be Mr. Moore. I expected you in today, but Tobias, our new junior clerk, must have been the one who came to collect. Let me write out a receipt for you right away. I trust you paid fifteen shillings six pence as usual?" asked Peter.

"Indeed I did, as usual," replied the man. Peter took out a ledger journal and wrote the receipt.

After Mr. Moore had left, Peter went directly to the daily receipt journal to check that the rent payment had been recorded. There was no entry that matched Mr. Moore's, but Peter did not want to think the worst. He would give Tobias the benefit of the doubt and wait for his return to the office. Perhaps he had taken the initiative and gone to retrieve the payment himself from the renter. Surely he was on this way back to the office at this very moment. Peter hung up his coat and removed his hat and hooked them on the wall next to his desk. He settled in to doing his clerk's work and to wait for Tobias to return. It was not long before he heard the front office door open. He quickly closed the ledger book so not to draw attention to the issue. He would draw out the truth from Tobias with some simple questioning.

"I just returned with the coal, and the fire has been stoked. The office has warmed up quickly. Was the cold too much for you to bear? Did you take a walk around the square to get the blood flowing again?" asked Peter, hoping to get Tobias to reveal the reason for his absence.

"Oh, yes that's where I was. The office was bone cold, and so I hiked about to get my body warmed up," replied Tobias without revealing any of the truth.

"Funny thing happened just before you returned; one of the tenant house renters was in saying he had a visit from someone from our office today."

"Oh, that's odd. He must have made a mistake in thinking it was someone from our office."

"I don't think so, and since I was only out myself today to fetch the coal, it could only have been you," said Peter, beginning to apply pressure for answers from Tobias. Feeling now that he had no choice, Tobias was compelled to tell Peter the truth.

"Okay, so what if I did collect the rent? No one will know the difference if we don't say anything. I tell you what, I'll split it with you, and we can keep this all to ourselves."

"Tobias, you may cut deals like that on the street, but now that you are in a position of responsibility and trust you can't expect to carry on that way."

"So you're going to make an honest man of me, are you?"

"Don't you want to better yourself? Mr. Scrooge has given you an opportunity to make a change. Don't you get that?"

"What I get is that I have a dying mother in a hospital that is killing her every day she remains there. I was going to pocket the money and use it to pay for private care for her so that she may stand a chance to survive," confessed Tobias, his eyes beginning to well up.

"I didn't know that your mother was sick, Tobias. I am very sorry to hear that. I can understand why you were drawn to take this action, but there are other ways to find the means to help your mother. You could have started by sharing this with Mr. Scrooge, and my father and me; we would have helped you," replied Peter.

"I did tell Uncle Ebenezer, but he didn't say or do anything about it," replied Tobias.

"If I know Mr. Scrooge, he may not have told you, but he would be planning something, Tobias, trust me. Right now the best thing for you to do is return the money you took. You will have to tell Mr. Scrooge what you did. Will you do what I suggest?" asked Peter, hoping that he would not have to convince Tobias any further.

"I know I must tell him, but I'm afraid he'll take it as a betrayal of his trust. He's done so much for me, and I've repaid him by stealing from him. I don't know how he can forgive me," replied Tobias, fearing the worst.

He had never experienced forgiveness before. It was an obscure virtue, not a reality in his world. He had never forgiven anyone else and found it impossible now to believe anyone would forgive him. Fear gripped him so that he could not think straight. He knew what he was supposed to do, but he could not break away from his old ways. He could not tell Ebenezer what happened today. He would do anything to get what he needed, even if it meant betraying the one who had just extended mercy to him. He knew it didn't make sense, but he could not bring himself to transform his thinking. He was still very much the street thief he had become over the years. It would take nothing short of a miracle to change that. Without him realizing it, a miracle of sorts had begun through his chance meeting with Ebenezer. With time it was possible for this miracle to take seed in Tobias' heart. It was this change of heart that Ebenezer needed in order to free Jacob from his bondage. Time, however, would not last forever. The twenty-fourth of December was drawing closer with each passing day.

Chapter 14

Their Mutual Acquaintance

Ebenezer escorted Belle out into the hall to speak with her privately.

"We deal with matters of life and death every day here. What specifically do you mean?" asked Belle with a slight tone of irritation.

"I am sorry for my abrupt approach, Nurse Pearce. My concern is for Mrs. Harding's well-being, and I believe you are the best person to assist in this matter."

"How do you mean?"

"I came here with the intent of assisting Mrs. Harding and arranging private care for her."

"Any one of our patients is in need of more care than we can provide."

"But if only she could receive your care, exclusively, I am certain that she would be restored to full health in no time."

"There's no doubt that if any patient had the full attention of any of the nurses, they would be far better off. That, unfortunately, is not possible. What did you have in mind?"

"Perhaps I can explain everything after you have finished your duties here for the day. Could we meet at the tavern across from the hospital when you are done?"

"I am most interested in hearing what you have to say, especially if it concerns the well-being of one of my patients. But it may not be appropriate that we meet privately, as I don't even know who you are."

"Well, that is not actually true. We do know each other from a time long past. Please meet with me, and I will explain everything."

"You say that I know you, but you do not look at all familiar to me. I must know where you came from in my past. I will agree to see you on one condition, that you give me the name of at least someone we knew in common when we first met."

Ebenezer wanted to tell Belle everything right there, but he knew that news like this was better delivered in more inviting surroundings. That is why he requested they meet at the corner tavern across the street. He knew he had to give her an answer to ensure her agreement to the meeting, but he did not want his identity fully revealed until they were alone sitting face to face. He could not give her a name that would be too obvious. The only name he could think of that might keep her guessing until they met was Mr. Fezziwig. They had met at his annual Christmas party with a room full of people she would have met for the first time that night as well. His name would have to do.

"All right then, we both know Mr. Archibald Fezziwig. Now, will you meet me after your shift is done across the street?" Ebenezer asked, hoping that it had satisfied her conditions.

"Mr. Fezziwig? I do not recall who he is or where I would know him from."

"Ah, but I have met your conditions by providing his name. It was not part of your provision that you need to actually remember who he was."

"True enough. I will agree to meet you after my work is finished here. I am not off for another two hours. That should give me enough time to place this Mr. Fezziwig and figure out who you are."

"If you do figure it out, you will still meet me at the tavern, even if you may not like who I am?"

"And why might I not like you? Have you done me harm, sir?"

"No harm that cannot be restored. I am not the man you knew me to be; I can assure you of that."

"Then I will certainly come and see if what you say is true."

"Then I will see you in two short hours. Please don't let me keep you from your duties. I need to speak briefly again with Mrs. Harding," Ebenezer said as he left Belle to attend to her work.

He walked up to Mrs. Harding's bedside and knelt down beside her so that his face was next to her ear. He placed the heather he had bought for her in her hands.

"Tobias is not bad; just bad things have happened to him, Mrs. Harding. He needs a strong father figure in his life. I know that I could never replace his birth father, your deceased husband, but I want to give Tobias a fighting chance to make it in this life. It is for that reason that I want to take on his guardianship. As his mother, you have the right to sanction my actions or withhold your endorsement. Either way, I will respect your decision concerning my intentions," replied Ebenezer. Mrs. Harding began to weep as she realized what he was asking of her.

"Never in my long, hard life have I known anyone who wanted to give of themselves as you do, Mr. Scrooge. I would like nothing more than for you to be Tobias' guardian. I know he is a good son, and he deserves the love and attention only a good father figure can give to him. I know that you are such a man, Mr. Scrooge."

"I only hope that I will be able to provide the guidance that Tobias needs. He loves you very much and wants to see that you can recover from your sickness. I want to help Tobias to that end, and so I will return soon and arrange for the kind of care that will assure your recovery."

"I have never met someone as kind as you; you have given me a hope that restores my soul. God bless you, Mr. Scrooge."

Ebenezer bid good-bye and then turned to leave. As he walked toward the ward room doors, a string of five metal chain links fell and landed at the foot of the bed. Mrs. Harding did not feel or hear them; Belle was busy attending to a patient at the far end of the room. The appearance of the chain links would go unnoticed until Mrs. Harding's bed was changed the next morning. By then there would be no one who could explain from where they came.

Chapter 15

Identities Revealed

Ebenezer had found the perfect table. It was tucked in behind the server's station, out of sight of most of the tavern guests. He had pre-selected a simple meal for the two of them so that no time would be wasted ordering. There was a great deal to discuss, and he wanted as much time as possible to spend engaged in dialogue with Belle. Just as the server delivered their mugs of hot cider, Belle appeared at the tavern entrance. Ebenezer waved to her and caught her attention immediately. He could see in her eyes that she had remembered him. The fact she still came gave him a rush of hope. She made her way over to the table, hung up her overcoat, and sat down across from him.

"Mr. Fezziwig was a good man. It was because of him that we met. For that I will be forever grateful," Ebenezer began gently.

"Is it obvious that I have remembered who he was, and who you are?"

"Yes, that is obvious, but what is not is whether you will still have anything to do with me, now that you know who I am."

"I must admit that when I first connected Mr. Fezziwig and you I was filled with deep sadness. I wasn't going to come. It was Mrs. Harding who convinced me to. You made a great impression on her. She could not stop talking about you and your intent to be the guardian of her son. It appears that you are again the Ebenezer I once knew. For years I held onto the belief that you could change back to being that man, but the belief faded with time. What happened to change you?" asked Belle.

"I will tell you the whole glorious story when we meet again, but it is a whole conversation on its own. Tonight, I want to talk about you. What happened after us? Did you ever marry?"

"After a time I moved on and managed to put you out of my mind, but I could never erase you completely from my heart. I did eventually meet someone, and we married. We had a child, a beautiful girl. We were happy for a time, but my husband fell ill and died suddenly, leaving me a widow, and I never remarried. After a while, I began to focus my life in new directions and found purpose and peace in caring for the needs of others. That is what led me into nursing, and I have been doing that now for over twenty years." She put her hand on his cheek.

"I never did stop loving you, Ebenezer."

"So you still have feelings for me?"

"Yes, they are still there, locked deep in my heart."

"Could they ever be unlocked once more?"

"Yes, I believe they could, but it will take some time. A neglected lock of forty years cannot be opened without a trusted key."

"May I suggest then, that we begin to build that trust starting now? And I know exactly where we can begin. I am holding a celebration at my home this Friday. I have called for this festivity to celebrate Tobias's homecoming. I can arrange for a carriage to bring you there at five o'clock. There is no formality at my gatherings. We celebrate with good food, fun, and music. All frowns and sad faces are required to be hung up and left at the front door!" laughed Ebenezer.

Belle smiled, trying to hold back, but Ebenezer's laugh was so contagious she could not resist and soon joined him with a full and uncontrollable laugh of her own. It had been longer than she could remember since she had laughed so. It felt exhilarating; her whole body relaxed and she felt good. After taking a deep breath and composing herself, she continued.

"Before we talk of homecomings and parties, you invited me here to talk about Mrs. Harding. A matter of life or death, I believe you said?" quipped Belle.

"Why, of course I did. How forgetful of me. This is what I brought you here in the first place to discuss. It most definitely concerns Mrs. Harding."

"Yes, it was about Mrs. Harding, but I am beginning to think you had other intentions in asking me here," replied Belle, wanting to appear annoyed.

"As you know, I will be her son's guardian. His only desire is to get his mother out of hospital and arrange for personal care for her. He does not have the means to pay for this, and so he has been stealing and cheating in order to collect enough to find the money. I took pity on him and promised to take care of the matter myself."

"Won't this be a significant expense to you?" asked Belle.

"I suppose. To me, money has become a means to help others. I have more than enough for my own needs, so keeping any more of it seems self-centred, don't you think?"

"Money has never had a hold on me, and it didn't have such a hold on you when we first met. I believe you are returning to be the man I knew and would have married."

"I believe I am, Belle. I have been blessed with an abundance of financial means, and I look for ways to pass on that blessing to others. So we come back to Mrs. Harding. Let me get straight to it. I would like you to take charge of her personal care. You can direct her care as you see fit. Whatever your compensation is from the hospital, it will be more than matched. In the meantime I will arrange for an apartment for Mrs. Harding."

"My, this is a surprise. We both know that she would be better off with bedside care from a dedicated private nurse. Any patient would benefit from such care, but there are few who can afford it."

"I will spare no expense and want the very best of care for her. That is why I want you to be her nurse."

"But you know I am regular staff at Charing Cross. I have been there for over twenty years and would have to make proper arrangements."

"Why of course that is understood. If it would help for me to speak with those in charge . . ."

"You really want me to do this for you, don't you?"

"Yes—for me, for Mrs. Harding, and especially for Tobias."

"You make it hard to say no. Let me think on it over night. I do want to help, but there is a great deal to consider."

"I understand. Take all the time you need. In the meantime, I will start looking for a proper place for Mrs. Harding to reside. Now, getting back to the party, when shall I have the carriage come around to pick you up?"

They continued to talk and reminisce all evening long. It was not until the tavern owner had sent the entire staff home and was blowing out all the candles that they noticed how late it was. The romance they once had was beginning to return. Over the next months their love for each other would become even stronger than it first had grown to be.

Chapter 16
The Plan

"This Mr. Scrooge must have a lot of nice things in his home, eh?" asked Tagger, hoping that Tobias would know where all the valuable and saleable items would be. The saleable items were more useful to them than the valuable ones. If they could not trade them quickly and easily there was no need in taking them. Paintings and fine furniture would be too difficult to turn into ready currency. They needed to go for jewels, gold, silver, and money.

"I haven't been through the whole house yet. I've only seen the main rooms on the ground floor, and my bedchambers, of course," replied Tobias.

"Do you have access to the whole house, or are there rooms you can't go into?"

"I was told I had full use of the house, and I haven't found a door yet that was locked."

"So then, what have you seen? You know what we usually go after. Any gold or silver?"

"No, not much. There was a silver tea set and a couple of gold-plated candlesticks."

"Hardly worth getting caught for. What about pound notes and coin? Where does he keep his money?"

"He may keep some of it in his bedchamber, but most likely it is at his office. It is a counting house, and I have seen a lot of cash money there."

"Why didn't you say so? That's what we'll do. Forget the house; let's do the office. It should be easier too. No one living there at night, I'm sure?"

"No, unless someone works late, but it never goes past nine o'clock."

"Anyone keeping an eye on the place after that, like a bobby on his night walk?"

"There may be some police patrolling those streets, but we should have no problem with them."

"Well then, I think we have ourselves a place to hit. All we have to decide is when. Have any ideas?"

"We're in luck. A party has been planned for tomorrow night. It's to celebrate my arrival, and the office is being closed early for the festivities. There will be no one at the office after five o'clock."

"Spot on! Then tomorrow night it is. You'll have to tell me where the strongbox is kept, and I'll need a key to get in."

"If you use a key it'll look like someone with access did the robbery."

"That's easy. I'll bust up the lock and handle with a chisel to make it look like it was a forced entry. Trust me, Tobias, this will be the easiest money you have ever made, and you won't even have to be there. While you're sippin' tea and eatin' crumpets at your party, I'll be clearing out Mr. Scrooge's office!" laughed Tagger as he danced a jig and snapped his fingers.

Tobias was not as happy as his street partner. He knew that this was a good plan and that he would get the money he was looking for. It was his conscience that was, again, interfering with his peace of mind. There was a part of him that knew that this was wrong, and he wanted to stop it. This newfound conscience, however, was not as strong as his thirst for money.

"Once you get the money, head for our secret meeting place. I'll come there after the party, around midnight tomorrow," instructed Tobias.

Any thread of righteousness was slipping away as he returned to his thieving ways. It seemed hopeless that he could ever have a change of heart. The same, however, would have been said about Ebenezer, and Ebenezer had found his redemption; Tobias could still find his.

Chapter 17

The Homecoming

Mrs. Nottingham had outdone herself this time. She had spent two days preparing the food for the celebration. Ebenezer had instructed her to spare no detail and to make this party the biggest and most memorable of all. Her hors d'oeuvres could awaken one's every taste bud, and she was quite skillful at knowing the exact entrée dish to pair with every kind of meat and finish with a display of dazzling sweets that marked a most memorable finale to a perfect feast. Ebenezer found any cause for a celebration and did it with a childlike delight. There had never been more laughter and song and joy in his home. It had become a place of amusement and playfulness. Everyone enjoyed Ebenezer's parties, and all his guests left a little lighter on their feet and a little younger in their heart.

Tonight the house was sparkling with excitement. Every candle in the house was lit, and there were fresh flower bouquets bursting with colour and exotic scents found in every room, on every floor. Ebenezer had hired a fiddler to make music the whole night through. He would play anything from a waltz to a Welsh jig and everything in between. The house came alive with all the sights, sounds, and smells of a festive cavalcade.

While dressing for the party, Ebenezer was thinking about the events that had taken place in these few short weeks since his second visit from Jacob. He was amazed at the pace at which chance encounters had been manifested. He believed he had made a difference in the lives of many of those he had met, but he had yet to see the kind of transformation that Jacob spoke of, the one that would spark a total change of heart in someone like the one he himself had experienced. Ebenezer hoped that a total transformation would take place soon, and he hoped it would be with Tobias.

He finished dressing and came down to the vestibule just in time to greet his first guests. The first to arrive were the Cratchits: Bob and his wife, Dorothy, and their children, Martha, Belinda, Mary, Charles, and Tiny Tim. Tiny Tim's legs looked good and strong, and he had such rosy cheeks. It overjoyed Ebenezer to see him in such good health. Next to arrive was his nephew, Fred, and his wife, Emily. They had grown wonderfully close in the past weeks, and Ebenezer had already become a favorite uncle to their three children. Ebenezer anxiously awaited the arrival of Belle. He had arranged for the carriage to pick her up promptly at five o'clock, which meant that she would be arriving any moment. Just then she walked in the front door and made her way directly to where Ebenezer was standing.

"Thank you for arranging transport for me. You have a charming and most inviting home, Ebenezer." Belle smiled as she said this.

"What makes it that way are the friends who grace it with their presence. Thank you so very much for coming," replied Ebenezer, returning the smile.

The guests began to pour in and now had to be directed by Mrs. Nottingham in order to avoid a congestion of bodies, coats, and hats. With little fuss, she managed to steer all newcomers to the cloak room and the rest into the dining room where they were instructed to begin serving themselves as they filed in one by one. The meal was served with military style efficiency but without one guest feeling rushed or overlooked. There was plenty of food for all; no one went hungry or lacked drink.

With bellies full and thirsts quenched it was time for some parlour games. One of Ebenezer's favourites was the name game. Everyone would write down a name on a piece of paper. It could be any name, either real or fictitious; someone from the past or in the present. Once everyone had written down a name and placed it in the hat, the names were then read aloud twice before the game began. The goal of the game was for each participant to guess the name of each of the other participants before someone else had guessed who they were. The last one left was the winner. The fun lay in the names chosen, and since one could choose virtually any name there was always an amusing array offered up. In the game this night, there were names like George Washington, Henry the VIII, Caesar Augustus, Noah, Joan of Arc, Macbeth, and Stanley the fishmonger. Tonight Ebenezer was in top form. The banter went back and forth between him and two other players for a while, but in the end Ebenezer was the victor. The name he used to win the game was Jacob, in honour of his deceased yet spirit-filled business partner. Belle played as well and reveled in seeing Ebenezer have such great fun trying to outwit his fellow opponents.

"I have never seen you have such fun and laugh so long as you did playing this delightful little game," whispered Belle as Ebenezer made his return from the centre of the room to join her on the window bench.

"It has never been near as fun without you here. I am my old self again, just as we were when we were courting. Where are my manners? A gentleman is always attentive to the woman he desires to impress. Your glass is empty; can I get you another?" asked Ebenezer, bowing down and kissing Belle's hand.

"Oh Ebenezer, you are just like you were as a young man, ever the one to make me smile and laugh. A second cup would be very nice; the punch was most delightful." Belle extended her arm to give Ebenezer her empty punch cup. He quickly returned with a full glass. As he presented the drink to her, he suddenly remembered something.

"Oh, I have almost forgotten. I have an announcement to make. Come with me!" Ebenezer took Belle's hand and led her to the top of the staircase that led to the second floor. From there they could look down on the vestibule. It was the best place from which to make his announcement. All that was required was to have someone assemble the crowd, and who better than Tobias. Tobias could both lead each guest to the appointed place and at the same time profit from the opportunity to introduce himself to them. Ebenezer realized that before he could ask him to take on this task, he must first speak with Tobias and share the news of his announcement.

"I need to find Tobias and speak to him about the guardianship," said Ebenezer, leaving Belle for a moment to search for Tobias. He found him in the parlour singing and dancing with some newfound friends.

"Tobias, I would like to speak with you about something very important; it cannot wait. Will you join me at the top of the stairs where we can have our conversation?" asked Ebenezer

"Why but of course, Uncle. I will be right there," replied Tobias. He ended the dance and came directly. He arrived at the top of the staircase to be greeted by Belle.

"I don't believe we have met, but I have heard a great deal of good things about you from Ebenezer. I am Belle. I look forward to getting to know you better. But right now Ebenezer has some very exciting news to share with you, so let me leave the two of you alone to speak for a moment." Belle disappeared down the stairs.

"Tobias, I know that there has been a lot that has happened in these past few weeks. You must be overwhelmed, but I want to assure you that you have a safe haven here. I have made it possible for you to come and live with me permanently, if you wish to."

"Wish to? Oh yes, Uncle, I do wish to."

"And I will be your permanent guardian. You will be like family."

"How can that be? I don't understand."

"I have spoken with my solicitor, and he has cleared this with the judge. Welcome to your new home, my boy." Tobias suddenly felt a sickness in the pit of his stomach, and he knew precisely where it had come from. He was struggling between the joy of being accepted as Ebenezer's family and being offered a permanent home and the guilt knowing what was taking place at Ebenezer's office that night. A battle of conscience was beginning to rage in him. He could not contain these opposing wills for long. One or the other would eventually win him over.

"Ladies and gentlemen." Ebenezer commanded attention as all the party guests assembled in his large vestibule. "Tonight's celebration is in honour of a young man who scarcely a fortnight ago was a stranger to all of us," continued Ebenezer. "I see that many of my good friends have joined us to celebrate Tobias Harding's coming to my home to live under my full and legal guardianship. The judge confirmed today with my solicitor, who I see standing right by the buffet table. Gerald did you get your fill of Mrs. Nottingham's roast beef?"

Mr. Striker acknowledged Ebenezer's remark with a wave of his hand and nod of his head. The guests all reveled in the news by clapping their hands and remarking with their support.

"I see that the whole Cratchit family has joined us. Tiny Tim, you look as healthy as a spring lamb, my boy! Wait, the whole Cratchit family is not present. Where is Master Peter?" asked Ebenezer as the guests looked at each other, searching for him.

"He is not here yet; he insisted on working late at the office. He had an account to finish tabulating," replied his father. Just as this was said, there was a commotion at the front door. In rushed Peter, accompanied by an officer of the law.

"Peter, we were just speaking about you. You have finally joined us. I am very surprised to hear that you were working late. Although I admire dedication, you do remember that I said everyone was to stop work today at five o'clock and come join us for the party?" exclaimed Ebenezer.

"I left the office as soon as I could. I was on my way here when I remembered that I had left a candle burning at my desk. When I returned to take care of it, I found the door open and I heard a noise inside the office. Instead of entering, I went to fetch a bobby to assist. When we returned, the office was empty. I went to check the strongbox first thing. I am sorry to have to tell you this, Mr. Scrooge, but we have been robbed and the strongbox is gone," Peter announced sadly.

"Have they caught anyone yet?" asked Bob Cratchit, directing his question to the constable who had arrived with Peter.

"In fact we have, sir. We are questioning him at the precinct right now, and it seems he was not alone in this," replied the constable. Tobias' face went ash white. He knew that if Tagger was offered a lesser sentence for a confession of who he was working with, he would take it. Tobias' fate now lay in the hands of an untrustworthy rogue who was at this very moment telling everything to the police.

Chapter 18

Tagger Takes the Offer

Tagger was seated at a simple wooden table in a musty room with no windows. With him in the room were two police officers firing questions at him one after the other.

"We have reason to believe that you did not do this alone. If you tell us who you worked with we can make this easier for you," barked one of the two officers towering over Tagger.

"What makes you think I couldn't do this on me own?"

"You aren't smart enough to pull this off yourself, Tagger. We both know that."

"What will you do for me if I do name someone?"

"With your record this could get you ten years in jail. If you cooperate, we can get that reduced to five."

"Some help that is. Five years is a lifetime, you know?"

"Ah, you're young. You have your whole life ahead of you. Think of this: you won't have to scrounge for food or a place to stay for five years."

"I know what it's like in there. Nothing is for nothing. They work you to the bone and feed you just enough to keep you useful to 'em. You have to do better than that if I'm going to help you."

"All right, if we could get you three years with, shall we say, a choice labour duty would that help you share with us your little secret?"

"How do you know I can trust you on that?"

"Seems to me you don't have much choice but to trust us. You've finally run out of options. You knew it would come sooner or later, didn't you?"

"All right. I suspect you might have ideas of your own about who would've been me partner in this one?"

"Well, in fact, we do. It's no secret that you and Tobias Harding have done a fair deal of damage together. Might he have been the one you did this with?"

"It's not hard to put that one together. I'm sure you know that he was workin' for Mr. Scrooge?"

"That was known to us, yes."

"So why didn't you bring him in yourself? You don't need me to convict him."

"Well, it makes our job easier if we have a confession. That's the deal, Tagger. You make it easier for us, and then we make it easier for you. Now let's talk about the whereabouts of the stolen money. How easy is that going to be to find out?"

"About as easy as it was giving you Tobias—I didn't get far with it. It's hidden in a spot that only I know of."

"Can you describe to us where that is?"

"I could, but then you'd know me spot. If you let me go, I could bring it to you straightaway."

"How do we know we could trust you not to escape?"

"Seems to me you don't have much choice but to trust me. Funny how trust has a way of repeatin' itself, isn't it?"

"We'll let you go get the money, but you won't be alone. We'll have an officer with you right to the building you have it hidden in."

The officer took Tagger by the arm and led him out into the main office of the precinct. Another officer was instructed what to do to accompany him, and they left moments later to retrieve the strongbox he had hidden earlier that night. Tagger would not miss his opportunity to escape. His plan was to cooperate with the officer until he was alone in the building where the strongbox was hidden. There was a hinged window too small for a grown man to fit through at the back of the building. His small frame would easily fit through it, and he would be long gone before the unassuming officer would realize that he had been duped.

Chapter 19

The Arrest

He knew it was only a matter of time before they came for him. So when they arrived at the counting house to arrest him, he gave them no resistance. Ebenezer was there in his office at the time and was the first one to speak to the police.

"Good day, officers. Have we reason for concern with your unexpected visit this morning?" asked Ebenezer, having no idea that they had come for Tobias.

"Mr. Scrooge, we have evidence and a testimony that gives us enough to charge Tobias Harding for the robbery at your office several nights ago," replied one of the officers. Ebenezer was overwhelmed by the news. He had never suspected Tobias, and he wanted to believe that Tobias would not have done this. He chose to give Tobias the benefit of his doubt.

"Tobias, can you explain what this is all about?" Ebenezer asked.

"There is no sense in denying the truth. I was involved with the robbery. Take me at your will." Tobias held out his hands, expecting to be put in chains.

"Please, officers, there is no need for those restraints. Tobias is going peacefully with you. I would like to accompany him, if I may," Ebenezer asked.

"Sorry, Mr. Scrooge, but the shackles are required, especially for a repeat criminal. There is always a concern of flight," replied the officer in charge.

"I can assure you that he will not attempt escape, officer. I am his guardian and take full responsibility for him. Tobias, get your coat. We are going with these gentlemen to the station. Once we are there, I will call for Mr. Striker. We will do all that we can to defend you on this, my boy."

Tobias could not believe Ebenezer still wanted to help him. If it was anyone else, Tobias would have been led away in chains and left to fend for himself. Despite knowing that Tobias was involved in the robbery, Ebenezer was still by his side. The fear he had about being rejected by Ebenezer seemed senseless now.

Everything had now changed. He was again on his way to jail with no present hope of release, and his plans to get his mother out of hospital would be all but vanished.

Chapter 20

The Sentence

It was the same courtroom he was last arraigned in, and it would be Judge Bartholomew presiding once again. This time there would be less formality and the judge would be short on mercy. Tobias was restrained and held by two court officers on either side. There was no crown attorney present, just the judge and court clerk. Ebenezer was seated in the gallery with his solicitor, Gerald Striker, next to him. Tobias' back was turned, so he did not see them enter the courtroom.

"Young man, I must say that I am not surprised to see you back in my court. I did, however, expect you to last a little longer than a fortnight. I signed the papers for your guardianship to Mr. Scrooge. Is he here in the court?" asked the judge, peering down at some papers on his desk. Ebenezer stood up to acknowledge his presence. Tobias turned and noticed for the first time that he was there as he promised he would be.

"Yes, your lordship, I am here as Tobias Harding's guardian."

"Your duties as a guardian have already been put to the test I see, Mr. Scrooge."

"If it pleases your lordship, I would like to explain the particulars."

"I don't see that there is much to explain, Mr. Scrooge. The police report is quite clear. There is circumstantial evidence and a signed testimony that indicate that Mr. Harding was an accomplice to the crime in question."

"Yes, so it appears; however, it was my property that was stolen, and I wish to withdraw my claim on this property and therefore exonerate Tobias from all and anything to do with the matter."

"Mr. Scrooge, it appears that you have been trained in the profession of litigation, or could it be that the gentleman seated beside you that may have given you counsel for your rhetoric?" replied the judge, growing agitated with Ebenezer and his continued defense of Tobias's felonies.

Mr. Striker had, in fact, given him a line of defense to use to release Tobias from the charge. He did, however, caution Ebenezer about the peril of doing so and counseled him to consider the consequences of continuing to discharge Tobias from the responsibility of his actions. Ebenezer now had to choose between extending to Tobias his unquestioning support and providing him with wise direction that would require a curative discipline.

"Your lordship, I only wish to defend the interests of the young man I have charge of."

"It would appear to me, Mr. Scrooge, that if you were interested in what would be best for this young man you would not continue to find feeble excuses in his defense but rather would consider giving the boy the kind of discipline a loving parent would give in order to correct his child's delinquent ways," insisted the judge. This charge struck Ebenezer profoundly, and he had no choice but to heed the judge's response. He knew that the best thing he could do for Tobias was to allow the court to give him a sentence and send him to jail for his own good.

"You give just commentary on this matter, your lordship, and I shall acquiesce to your judgment. I only ask that you pass a fair sentence that may correct and not damage his young spirit."

"I will take your request into consideration, Mr. Scrooge, but he must receive punishment for his actions."

"If it pleases the court, I only ask that you not bring down the severest of sentences."

"For this crime alone the court could bring down a full sentence of five years of hard labour. Mr. Harding has committed many other crimes that have gone unpunished, and so it is the decision of this court that with all being considered, including Mr. Scrooge's appeal for leniency, he shall receive no less than three years. I will allow for his sentence to be served in a provisionary facility closest to the city," stated the judge, slamming his gavel down twice with a firm gesture. Ebenezer was unclear what the judge had actually said. Mr. Striker explained to him that a provisionary facility was more of a farm than a prison. They were established to provide food for all the prisons throughout England. They would have grain fields, livestock, and gardens, all farmed by the prison's inmates. It was a far less arduous type of labour and was a kindness extended to Tobias by the judge. Tobias, however, did not have the advantage of Mr. Striker's explanation and only heard and understood that he was being sent to prison for three years. He could not understand why Ebenezer did not protest harder. He could have convinced the judge to place him back into Ebenezer's custody as his guardian. Three years was an eternity to him. What made it worse was the fact that Tagger was off free enjoying the spoils of the crime that Tobias was now paying for with this three-year sentence. His anger increased with this thought running through his mind.

Ebenezer was surprised at the length of the sentence but thankful that Tobias would be in a more benevolent environment. The farm would be a good place for him to learn and mature. On the advice of Mr. Striker, Ebenezer decided that he would petition the court for a shorter sentence once Tobias had been in for a period and was exhibiting reformed behaviour.

The judge rose and signaled the court officers to take Tobias away to the holding cell where he would be prepared for his transfer to the provisional facility, which was an hour's ride from London. As Tobias was led from the courtroom, Ebenezer approached him.

"Tobias, I know that this must seem a harsh punishment, but be encouraged. I have been told that the provisional facility is a better place than any other. You will be farming, which is good and honourable work. And I will come to visit you every week," said Ebenezer, looking Tobias caringly in his eyes.

"I don't want you coming near me ever again. Thanks to you I'm being put away for three long years. You could've convinced the judge to release me to you, but instead you let him sentence me to prison. I thought you cared about me," replied Tobias angrily.

He turned away from Ebenezer as he was led out of the courtroom and out of sight. Ebenezer was crushed by Tobias' response. He sincerely thought he was doing what was best for him. Now it seemed he had driven Tobias further away. Ebenezer wondered if he had, perhaps, just extinguished the only chance of helping him experience a true change of heart.

Chapter 21

Mrs. Harding Comes to Stay

A month had passed since Tobias was placed in the prison. It was not the type of prison with walls that kept prisoners from escaping. Instead there were guards who accompanied the inmates as they went about their duties. Tobias had been assigned to milking the herd. He had become quite accomplished at filling the milk bucket, but it had not come without a requisite kick in the shins and countless spills.

Ebenezer had come to see Tobias on several occasions, but Tobias had refused to see him each time. The ride from London was an hour each way, but Ebenezer refused to relent. He made the trek out to the prison every week, and each week Tobias refused to meet with him. Ebenezer vowed to continue returning in the hope that Tobias would eventually relinquish his silence.

In the meantime, Ebenezer went about his business, always looking for someone to help and possibly assist in their heart's transformation. This particular day he was going to visit Mrs. Harding to make good on the promise he had made to Tobias. He had decided with Belle that Mrs. Harding would come and live with him. He had looked at many places for her, but none were ideal. In the end, he determined that the best place for her was with him, right under his roof. There was a perfect room on the main floor that had been used for a study. It had long been left empty, and so with just a few additions and a thorough cleaning, the room was easily transformed into a comfortable bedroom for her. Belle had arranged to be her day nurse and had even arranged it with Mrs. Nottingham that she could continue working a reduced shift at the hospital. Mrs. Nottingham would see to it that Mrs. Harding received her meals and would act as her attendant during Belle's absence. Everything had been arranged. The only remaining task now was to bring her home from the hospital. Ebenezer arrived just in time. Belle was having a little difficulty convincing Mrs. Harding of their plans.

"Mrs. Harding, this will be the best for you. You will receive my personal care in the comfortable surroundings of Mr. Scrooge's home," explained Belle.

"But I don't want to be a burden to Mr. Scrooge's household. I will just get in the way."

"I don't see how you could get in anyone's way, Mrs. Harding. I have a half-empty house. With you living in it with me I won't feel guilty that is goes unused. You will be doing me a kind favour, so I insist you come and live with me. It will just be until you are completely well. After that you can choose to stay or find an apartment of your own," replied Ebenezer in a convincing tone.

"Well, if it is only until I recover, I don't see any harm in that. You are most generous, Mr. Scrooge, to open your home to me," replied Mrs. Harding.

"I did it for your son, and I can most certainly do it for you, Mrs. Harding," insisted Ebenezer.

He took her gently by the hand and helped her on with her coat. Belle assured her that she would be along shortly to help her settle in. As Ebenezer walked with her arm and arm toward the exit, Belle thought to herself how good and kind he had become. He was surely the man she remembered him to be before the love of money had seized his heart. As they disappeared through the ward room doors, she began to imagine how magnificent her life would be as the wife of Ebenezer Scrooge.

Chapter 22

The Devil's Pit

Each week Ebenezer continued to go to see Tobias, and every week he would return without being allowed a visit. He was not discouraged, however, as he was determined to find a way through to Tobias. Ebenezer turned to other munificent activities to keep his mind off of the situation. One such important activity, and one he had not forgotten about, was the clandestine visit that he was to arrange to a child labour factory with the prime minister. The prime minister himself had not forgotten. It was his personal secretary who sent Ebenezer a note that requested that he arrange a meeting at a "previously discussed location." It was not hard for him to choose the factory to take him to. He could have chosen one of a hundred in the city limits of London and several hundred more throughout the adjoining municipalities.

His choice was known as Devil's Pit. The proper name was Hampton House. At one time it was a respected establishment that was run by a family of silversmiths. They produced silverware of the highest quality found nowhere else in His Majesty's dominion. Over the years, however, their standards had fallen and the demand for inexpensive flatware had allured the company's owners into running a factory that could produce significant volumes. In order to keep the production costs to a minimum, they employed children to provide the heavy labour required for such an operation. The working conditions were among the worst in all of England. Metal smelters ran continuously, creating intense heat. The workers had to pull coal railcars from the outside yard where the large supply of coal was situated to locations deep within the factory walls. The coal was destined for the furnaces that generated the fire required to melt the alloys. It was grueling and treacherous work. The shifts were twelve hours long with only seven hours respite between. Bunk houses had been erected for all the workers to sleep on site so that a minimum amount of time was spent traveling to work.

The two men arrived unannounced early one morning just as the shift had begun. Ebenezer minced no words with the men in charge.

"We are here on official government business to observe the working conditions of this establishment. My name is Ebenezer Scrooge, and if you check your company records you will find that I hold the mortgage paper on this property. As such, I have the legal right to inspect the premises at any time I deem suitable. And I find this morning quite suitable," instructed Ebenezer with a confident authority.

"I don't know what you came to observe here. We run a compliant operation. We haven't broken any laws," replied the foreman in charge.

"We are not looking for your compliance to the current laws, sir. On the contrary, we are looking to observe the working conditions in order to modify the laws to better protect child laborers," interjected the prime minister, not wanting to reveal his identity.

"Well, I suppose I have no choice but to comply with your wishes. I expect you will provide me with a full written report on your findings?" asked the foreman.

"We most certainly will. I will see to it that you are the first to receive a copy," replied Ebenezer.

He knew that any report resulting from this visit would most likely spark a firestorm of debate in Parliament. Ebenezer's hope was that it would not end in meaningless rhetoric but would lead to the full abolition of child labour throughout the Empire. They began their tour by visiting the children closest to the smelters. The coal was delivered to within yards of the burning furnaces where they stood shoveling. There seemed to be no end to their stoking of the furnace as the coal railcars lined up behind them beyond sight. There was molten metal from the smelters spilling out and splashing on the factory floor. The sizzling pieces struck the shoeless feet of the children. Their skin was black with soot and airborne ash. There was not one who was smiling. Only despondent expressions hung on their tiny faces. The prime minister was the first to speak with one of the children.

"How long have you been working at this, young man?" he asked.

"I lost me mom and dad to debtor's prison four years back. I haven't seen 'em or any of me family since then," answered the little boy.

He looked the same age as Tiny Tim, or so Ebenezer thought. He was only seven years old, three years younger than Tiny Tim. Most children looked older than they were due to the harsh conditions and the lack of basic care. If they remained in the workhouses throughout their childhood, the majority would not reach their eighteenth birthday.

"You described the conditions most accurately, I'm afraid Ebenezer," said the prime minister.

"And there are many more factories I could show you that would cast a confirmatory light on this place," replied Ebenezer.

"I see no need to look any further. I believe I have seen enough, Ebenezer."

"So are you now of the same opinion on this matter, James?"

"Without a doubt, there is just cause for concern for the well being of our nation's children."

"What will be your next course of action?"

"Let us arrange for several more visits to other factories and mines over the next while, and once we complete our findings I will table our report with the House. If this runs the course of time that my slave labour bill did, we may not see a full and final end to this injustice until sometime next year."

"Then let's be off to record and file our findings. We don't have a moment to lose," affirmed Ebenezer.

It would take some time before the abolition of child labour would be enacted, but its genesis was marked that day. It was Ebenezer's genuine compassion that was its spark. As they bid good-bye to the children with a promise to return, they did not notice several chain links appear and fall directly into the smelting fire. They were consumed instantly and left no trace.

Chapter 23
The Vicar's Advice

The months seemed to slip by and with them passed Ebenezer's hope of finding the one heart he needed to transform. He still believed that Tobias would be the one, but with him in prison and not speaking to Ebenezer, the chances of that happening drew fainter and fainter.

Ebenezer had promised himself that he would accomplish what only he could for Jacob. He knew he could not fail at this task, and the burden of it was becoming too much for him to bear. He had no peace of mind with it in his thoughts night and day. Every person he met was a candidate to him for reform. When they did not respond to his sincere intent, it would send him sliding back into despair. And, it followed him into his dream world every night. He had the same dream over and over again. In the dream he was standing before the gates of Heaven. He was denied entry because of his failure to find the one person that would allow Jacob to intervene in the lives of the living. Jacob stood at the gate staring at him with angry intensity.

"You said you would find the person to guide in their heart's transformation. You have failed me Ebenezer. I thought you were my friend," whined Jacob. That was where the dream would end each time. Those words from Jacob haunted him. Every waking hour they would echo in his mind to the point he could not take it anymore. If he did not get some help, he knew he would go mad. The question was where and from whom would he get help. He could not share this with just anyone. Not everyone would understand, and there were those he would not want to know.

One evening after the work day was finished, he decided to take a walk and clear his mind of the matter. He wondered the emptying streets of London going in any direction his whim would take him. He walked and walked until his feet went numb. Not able to go any further, he sat down on a bench to rest and to catch his breath. He crossed his leg and rested it on his knee to make it easier to remove his one shoe. He repeated the maneuver with his other leg, and then leaned back on the bench to stretch out his legs. He still couldn't feel his toes, so he started wiggling them to bring back the blood flow. Within a few minutes he was starting to feel the return of circulation to his feet. He sat gazing at the buildings that surrounded him. It was getting dark, and he had wondered into a neighbourhood he was not familiar with, but he felt safe and undaunted. Across the street directly in front of him was a small church that looked empty except for one room on the upper floor. There was a candle burning in the room casting a shadow of a person seated at a desk. Ebenezer figured it must be the church's vicar preparing for his Sunday service.

As Ebenezer sat gazing at the shadowy figure, the idea came to him to go and speak with whoever it was in that room. It had been a long time since he had stepped foot inside a church and even longer since he had spoken to a church clergy, but for some reason he knew he had to follow his feelings. He put on his shoes and walked across the street to the entrance to the church. The door was unlocked, so he entered and followed the light up the stairs to the upper room. When he reached the head of the stairs the man who was seated writing in the room must have heard him coming, and came out to greet him.

"Good evening sir, are you lost or looking for anyone in particular" asked the vicar in a gentle voice.

"I could be," replied Ebenezer. His answer puzzled the vicar.

"So you are lost, and looking for someone to guide you?" he asked.

"You could say that, and you just may be the one I was sent here to speak to. My name is Ebenezer Scrooge, and I came upon your church by chance this evening."

"I have come to believe that there is nothing that happens by chance. Everything, in one way or another, has the hand of God guiding it. Pleasure to meet you Mr. Scrooge. I am Vicar Wren. My friends call my Christopher"

"The pleasure is all mine, and please call me Ebenezer. So, you truly believe that God has an interest in the details of our lives? I imagined he was too busy stopping wars and ending plagues, and had no time to consider the particulars of anyone's life."

"There was a time when I, too thought like you do now, but I have seen far too many lives changed when one comes to know him. He is like a friend, and a good friend always cares about those he knows."

"You talk as if God is real and approachable, as if he was a man."

"Yes, I do because he is real if you choose to seek him in that way."

"What I believe I came to seek was peace; and the end to my torment. Can he give me that if I seek him?"

"Yes, you can find peace, and rest from all your troubles by knowing God."

"Then tell me how I can know him. Do you have to introduce me?"

The vicar laughed and put his hand on Ebenezer's shoulder.

"I can introduce the two of you to each other; that is part of my job," he chuckled.

"But first tell me about why you came to me this night. God works through willing helpers, and I have been helping him most of my life. He wants me to help you too, if you want to be."

Ebenezer began explaining all of the details from the very beginning. How Jacob had come to him, and how his life was changed forever by the visit of the three Christmas spirits.

Then he shared how Jacob had returned to give him a chance to alter the condition of Jacob's spirit by finding someone to help in the transformation of their heart. He told the vicar how Tobias had come into his life, and how circumstances had led to Tobias' rejection. He explained how earnestly he was trying to accomplish what was becoming seemingly impossible to him. It was this that was causing his anxiety, and was this that led him to the vicar's church this night.

"You have truly had a rebirth of your mind and soul, Ebenezer. You are a new man in every sense of the word," observed the vicar.

"Then why do I feel as I do, so weary and troubled," asked Ebenezer.

"It seems to me that you have only discovered half of the puzzle to a peace filled life"

"What do you mean?"

"What I mean is this-God has said in his word that there are two great commands to live by in this life. The one you have embraced like no one else I have ever met. That command is to love your neighbour as yourself. The other command, however, precedes the one you have discovered, and that is to love your God with all your heart soul and mind. God wants to have a personal relationship with you, Ebenezer. He wants you to give him all of your worries and troubles, and he wants you to trust him to guide your path."

"That sounds all well and good for a learned man like you, but I really have no idea what that looks like for someone like me."

"You aren't the first to tell me that. I know this is a concept that is quite strange and mysterious to most people. I tell you what, let us make arrangements for you to come back and visit with me. I will share with you stories of how others have come to know him as a trusted friend, and together I will help you to get to know him yourself," suggested the vicar.

With some reluctance, Ebenezer agreed to return. He was uncertain what this idea of knowing God was all about, but he did feel more at peace after spending time in conversation with the vicar. Ebenezer never considered himself a spiritual man, but there was now no denying that there was a spiritual realm. He could no longer explain away the super natural, and to deny the existence of a higher being would be a narrow minded view of the new world he had come to know since his first visit from Jacob.

He began the long walk back home with a renewed sense of hope. He was no closer to finding the one soul's heart to transform, nor any closer to seeing Tobias' transformation, but he did have a new confidence that came from knowing he was not in his quest alone.

Chapter 24

The Proposal

As the months past, Ebenezer's concentration remained on his one task, yet he managed to give Belle all of his remaining devotion. It was nearly a year since they were reunited by chance at Charing Cross. Ebenezer knew from the moment he saw Belle that day that his love for her had not died. Being with Belle this past year had made him the happiest he had been since their first engagement. He had lost her the first time; he would not lose her again.

He planned the evening so as not to alert Belle to his intentions. They were to meet for an evening meal at an unassuming tavern at the edge of Hyde Park. He thought that they would take a stroll before dinner to give him an opportunity to ask the question. He stood by the bridge where they had arranged to meet. It was precisely three minutes past the hour when she came into sight. His heart skipped a beat when his eyes met hers. He ran to her and gave her a loving embrace. "It is so good to see you. I missed you all day," exclaimed Ebenezer.

"But we were together just yesterday evening. Did you miss me that much in such a short time?" replied Belle.

"I must confess that I have been waiting to be with you and to ask you something that has been on my mind for some time." Ebenezer took Belle by the hand and sat her down beside him on a nearby bench. "I know that our reunion after all these years has come upon us rather suddenly and you may not yet be ready to entertain anything more, but I want you to know that I have feelings for you that require my endearing expression. I feel like I will burst if I cannot release these words to your tender ear."

"Please do, my dear Ebenezer. I too have feelings to express to you."

"I know that the man I was the day I left you is no longer alive but is gone forever. You have seen not through my words but through my deeds that I am a changed man."

"Yes, I truly see and know that you are, once again, that kind and loving man I met a lifetime ago."

"Then why don't we begin again at that moment where I, on bended knee, said this to you?" Ebenezer stood up and, taking Belle's hand, kneeled down with his eyes gazing into hers. He said, "Belle, you are the only woman I have ever loved and will ever love. My heart is yours. Will you take it and care for it and be my heart's desire from this moment on?"

Belle could not hold back her tears of joy. It was a joy only felt with a life's hope fulfilled. Her answer was yes. It was the only answer that she could give, for Ebenezer was again the man she had fallen in love with and was still in love with now. They embraced tenderly and held each other without speaking a word for what seemed hours.

With their two hearts reunited and their mutual desire to be together now revealed, their conversation moved naturally to the plans of marriage. They both agreed that a long engagement at their age was not necessary. They would have married the next day if it weren't for the sensible details that made for a proper wedding. Belle desired to have the wedding she had dreamed of when they were first engaged. It would be a wedding of silk and lace; of sweet laughter and tender tears. Ebenezer would make certain that it was the kind of wedding that most brides only dream of. It was one week until Christmas Eve. What better occasion than this night to celebrate their union? They would start making the necessary arrangements the next morning, and in seven days they would be married.

Chapter 25

In the Judge's Chambers

One thing Ebenezer had learned from the church vicar was that he was to pray as if everything depended on God and act as if everything depending on him. The wedding presented itself as an opportunity to get through to Tobias, and he knew it was now time for him to take action. With Mr. Striker's assistance, he arranged a meeting with Judge Bartholomew. It had been close to a year since Tobias began his sentence. In actual fact it was closer to ten months than a year, but he expressed it that way to the judge so that it would seem longer. He had come to ask the judge for an early release for Tobias. Mr. Striker thought Ebenezer's chance of convincing the judge to reduce his sentence from three years to one was unlikely. However, he did not discourage Ebenezer but instead offered to accompany him and show his support.

"We thank you for seeing us on short notice this morning, your lordship," began Ebenezer as they took a seat across from the judge, who was sitting at his desk. His chambers were small yet imposing. There was a large bay window that looked down one floor to the street level below. Dark oak paneling clad the chamber walls. Bookshelves stood along the length of the wall behind the judge's desk filled with legal journals neatly arranged by title and date.

"I understand that you have come to petition for the release of young Mr. Harding?"

"Yes your lordship, we have. If you check the prison warden's records I believe you will find that Tobias' behaviour has been exemplary this past year."

"Has it been a year since he was placed in . . . where was it we sent him to?"

"You sentenced him to three years at a provisional facility close to the city. That was a kind act of mercy on your part, your lordship."

"Oh, yes, now I remember. I heard he was given the duty of milking the herd, wasn't he?"

"Yes in fact he was. He has done a fine work of it."

"You would like that I would authorize his early parole; is that it?"

"Your lordship, I have taken a special interest in Tobias. I took pity on him, and I do believe that I can be the agent of his reform."

"Have you reason to believe that his incarceration over this past year has had any effect to that end, Mr. Scrooge?"

"I would like to believe so, but I have not been able to speak a word with Tobias since the day you sentenced him, your lordship."

"Why is that? Would the prison authorities not let you see him?"

"I wish it were that simple. It is Tobias who has refused to see me."

"I see. He was bitter that you allowed him to go to prison without intervening?"

"It appears so. If I could just get him to speak with me, I believe I could help him sort all this out between us."

"What makes you believe that he will speak to you out of prison when he refused to while in?"

"I am getting married the day after tomorrow. If I can get Tobias to the ceremony then I know I stand a chance that he will yield to reason. It is the only chance left before it is too late."

"Too late for what Mr. Scrooge?"

"Too late to make a difference."

"You have a firm resolve it seems in this matter. I respect your judgment, Mr. Scrooge. Your reputation as an advocate for reform has not gone unnoticed. I will grant you your request, but it will only be for a temporary release. He will have to serve at least one more year of his full sentence. I will release him on his own recognizance for two days in order for him to attend your wedding."

"Thank you, your lordship. You don't know the countless lives your decision may have an impact on."

"One thing is for certain—we expect that it will have a profound impact on the life of your young Mr. Harding."

"I am counting on it. And I am eternally grateful to you, your lordship." Ebenezer concluded with these words of gratitude, not realizing their prophetic implications. For indeed if he was able to convince Tobias to come there was a fighting chance that he could finally lead Tobias into making that crucial heart's transformation.

Ebenezer knew that there was precious little time left, for in two short days it would be Christmas Eve. He turned his full attention immediately to the most critical task at hand. He had to find a way to get Tobias to come to the wedding.

Chapter 26

Hope Fading

The only person he could think of who could convince Tobias to come was Mrs. Harding. The only issue was that she was not fit to make the two-hour return trip by carriage to the prison. Mrs. Harding had done very well over the past months she had been at Ebenezer's home, and they expected her to have a full recovery within a short time, but not soon enough. She was planning to attend the wedding ceremony, and this would be taxing enough on her with only a short ride from Chesterfield Hill to St. Paul's Cathedral.

There was little time left to reach Tobias before midnight the next day. Ebenezer knew that if Tobias refused to come, then all hope would be lost. The only other one Ebenezer could think of was Belle. She had made a connection with Tobias before he was sent away. He trusted her as his mother's nurse and, perhaps would be open to her requests. Ebenezer and Belle were together in his office making their final plans when he asked her.

"I know he will not see or listen to me, but he may with you."

"I am not sure of that, but we must try. I will do whatever you need of me, my dearest."

"Thank you, darling. I will have a carriage drive you out to see Tobias this afternoon. If you can just get him to come to the church, I know that it can be accomplished."

"What is it you are talking about?"

"Oh my, with all the flurry and fuss this past week I have not found the right moment to share with you the entire story, have I, my dear?"

"You have stories, many of which I have yet to hear, but we have a lifetime to share them with each other. If I know you, this has something to do with the well-being of another. That is all I need to know for now."

"You are an amazing woman, Belle. I have been blessed from above to have you as my wife."

"Well, I'm not your wife yet, and if I don't get these last details finished, I may not be your wife by tomorrow!"

"Quite right! Then finish up here and I will go summon you a carriage straightaway," Ebenezer replied with a loving squeeze of her hand.

By the time the carriage arrived, Belle had managed to tie up most of the loose ends of the wedding day plans.

"There, I feel much better. Now I can turn my attention to an equally important task. What should I do and who should I speak with when I arrive?" asked Belle, looking for direction from Ebenezer.

"You will want to speak with the warden, Mr. Frank. He is a kindly man. Explain the situation and ask him to bring Tobias to the visitation room by only saying that a woman has come to see him."

"Will that work? Will he agree to meet me by revealing only that?"

"I am quite sure it will work. For this entire past year, I have been the only would-be visitor to come and see Tobias. His curiosity will be piqued when he is told that a woman has come to see him. As long as it is not me, I'm sure he will agree to see most anyone."

"If he does agree to see me, what do I tell him?"

"Belle, you will know what to say. Tell him that the arrangements have been made for his temporary release to come to the wedding and that you would very much like him to attend. I don't think he will be able to refuse you."

"Should I mention anything about his mother?"

"I think not. I want him to be surprised when he sees her at the church. If you must tell him that his mother will be coming to convince him, then you must, but if he agrees with only your asking then say nothing more," concluded Ebenezer. Belle gathered her things and followed Ebenezer out to the street where her carriage was waiting. Ebenezer gave the instructions to the driver and then paid him.

"I need to believe that Tobias will not refuse your request. If he does agree to come, wait for him to pack his things, and bring him back with you. I have made arrangements for him to stay overnight with the Cratchits, so you can have the driver take him directly there upon your return," requested Ebenezer as he helped Belle up into the carriage.

As she drove away he said a prayer under his breath in hopes that what he believed would come true, that Tobias would be at the wedding and his heart's transformation would take place there. Belle was now his only hope.

Chapter 27

Belle's Plea

The carriage ride to the prison was long and uneven. The early winter was taking a toll on the road, and it would not be until the following spring that any of it could be repaired. Belle chose to ignore her discomfort and focused on her pending duty. She knew that Ebenezer was depending on her to bring Tobias to his senses.

It must have been hard for Ebenezer to drive every week to the prison, and to have felt Tobias's rejection each time. Belle, now truly felt his pain and frustration as her thoughts focused on the encounter with Tobias, and she believed that Ebenezer's unwavering diligence would not go unrewarded. For his sake, she knew she had to return successful.

Suddenly, she heard a knock on the carriage roof. It was the driver's signal to her that they had arrived. She put on her hat and placed her hat pin in its proper place. As she was putting on her lace gloves, the driver opened the door and placed a stepping stool on the ground to help Belle from the carriage. As she took her first step to descend, he offered his hand to guide her safely to the ground.

"Your driving was exemplary despite the rough condition of the road, Sir" remarked Belle to the driver as she made her way to the entrance of the prison.

"Thank you Mame. I trust you aren't too rattled from the ride? I did try and go easy on you." replied the driver.

"Why no, I have had worst rides, and survived. You will have to do better than that to rattle me!" exclaimed Belle. "I will be, I imagine, no more than an hour. I have come to convince a young man to follow his conscience, and his heart. If it takes longer than an hour, I fear he will never make the decision I came here for.

Please wait for me. If I return with a young man by my side, you will know I have succeeded in what I came here for today. If I return alone, then I'm afraid all hope will have been lost."

"I will believe for the best, Mame. It would be my pleasure to return to London with an additional passenger." The driver returned to the carriage to attend to his horses as Belle made her way into the prison entrance.

The prison was an old structure with solid oak beams, limestone walls and cobbled floors. Beyond the foyer there were iron gates that appeared to separate the prison offices from the rest of the compound. Beyond the iron gates there were four hallways that seemed to extend deep within the prison walls.

Belle looked for a guard who could help her in locating Tobias, but no one appeared to be in sight. At the far left corner of the foyer, a door was slightly ajar. A beam of light from the office shone through the door crack. Belle heard a rustling of papers, and made her way to the office entrance to knock. Before she could, a man dressed in a dark coloured uniform appeared from behind the door.

"Good day to you Mame. Have you been waiting long to be attended to?" asked the man in a professionally polite manner.

"Oh no, I just arrived actually. I was told to ask for Mr. Frank the prison warden."

"At your service, but please call me Harry. We like to do away with all the formalities here. We find it makes the inmates feel less like a prisoner, and more like a contributing member of our farm."

"That sounds quite wonderful. You must find that they are less disruptive and more content being here even if it is a prison?" asked Belle.

"Yes, most turn out that way. Very few have to return to us once they have completed their sentence."

"You have a most remarkable facility. If only all our prisons in England worked as yours does, you could put yourself out of work"

"And I would like nothing more than to do that. Now tell me what has brought you out on such a wintery cold day, Miss . . . ?"

"Belle Pearce, soon to be Scrooge."

"Oh, you must be Mr. Ebenezer Scrooge's bride to be?"

"Yes, in fact we are to be wedded tomorrow."

"Tomorrow? If I could be so bold to ask, but what are you doing here the very day before your wedding, Miss?"

"That, Harry is a good question. I have come to convince Tobias Harding that he needs to end his sentence of silence he has imposed on my Ebenezer over this past long year."

"I know, I have seen Mr. Scrooge come week after week without a chance to speak given to him by Tobias. I am sure it has been difficult to accept."

"Yes it has been a burden to carry for him. A burden I pray to end today. I would like to speak with Tobias. Is he free to meet with me?"

"I do believe they have finished their morning chores and are probably just ending their mid day meal. Can I have one of my guards bring him for you?"

"Yes, please. However, Ebenezer specifically requested that my name not be mentioned. Only to say that a woman was here to see him."

"Understood, Mame. Please make yourself comfortable in the room next to mine, and I will go make the necessary arrangements for you to see Tobias," requested Mr. Frank as he made his way behind the locked iron gates.

Belle stepped into the room and noticed there were only two chairs and a small square table separating them. She sat down on the chair next to the window. The mid day light felt warm on her face. She began to run the words she wanted to say to Tobias in her mind hoping that the practice would help her to relax and focus on the moment of engaging him.

Mr. Frank appeared at the entrance to the room only moments later with Tobias by his side. Tobias recognized Belle immediately, and ran to her with his arms wide open.

"You are a sight to see. I have seen no one that I know this past year while here. Next to my mother, I would have chosen you to be that one to see. How are you Belle?!" cried Tobias smiling with joy.

"I am a most content woman, Tobias. This past year has been filled with blessings beyond my thinking. There is only one thing that is yet to be fulfilled for me to have complete contentment."

"Please tell, what blessing is lacking, and what others have come your way?"

"They all have one thing in common, and pertain to the one I love. It is for Ebenezer I come to see you today, and it is for Ebenezer I pray you will listen to me now."

"His name and his betrayal are the only things that I have tried to erase from my memory all this past year." Tobias was noticeably agitated. His face became fire red, and he began to pace nervously back and fourth in the tiny room.

"Tobias, you do know Ebenezer has come to see you every week since you have been here, and you refused to speak to him every time?"

"Yes, I know. I have nothing to say to him. I never want to see him again."

"He did not betray you. He only wanted what was best for you."

"The best for me? I'm in prison. Is that the best thing for me?"

"Yes, I do believe it is right now. You know you did something that was wrong. You need to recognize what you did and take responsibility for your actions, Tobias."

"He could have insisted with the judge. The judge would have listened to him, but he let me go to prison. And in prison I'm helpless to do anything to get me mother out of hospital. He even promised to help me with her. Not only did he betray me, he's lied to me too." Belle wanted to tell Tobias what Ebenezer had done for his mother, but she remembered what he had asked her to do, and decided to remain silent. It was clear that Tobias was still bitter towards Ebenezer; perhaps more than ever. She had to approach this now in a different way. Tobias had always liked her, and it was clear he still had warm feelings for her. She decided she would use this as a final ploy to accomplish her task. She had nothing left to lose.

"You asked me what blessings I have had this year. The greatest one is that I am to be married." Belle changed the discussion to focus on her and Tobias' mother.

"Married, how wonderful. I do hope you have found someone else to marry?" replied Tobias sarcastically.

"There is only one for me, and we are to be married tomorrow, Christmas Eve. I would like to invite you to come see me be married Tobias. I want you to do it for me, not for Ebenezer."

"But how can I come, I am here and can't leave. My sentence is not nearly over yet."

"I have made arrangements for that. You have been given a pass to come to the wedding with the understanding that you must return two days hence."

"Why did you do that? It wasn't you who made the arrangements, it was him wasn't it?"

"Does it matter how the arrangements were made. You will have two days to come to the wedding, and see your mother as well. Surely that is worth it alone to see your mother again?"

Belle had struck a chord with Tobias. He would put aside his loathing of Ebenezer those two days to gain time with his mother. He would go to the wedding only for Belle.

"If I can see my mother, then I will go. When do we leave?"

"As soon as you can gather your things. A carriage is waiting for us at the prison entrance. You can stay with the Cratchits, everything has been arranged."

Tobias signaled to the guard to take him to his room. He came back a short time later with a satchel filled with enough for his two-day release. Belle took his arm and walked with him to the carriage. The driver noticed Belle returning with her anticipated companion.

"We have a full carriage returning to London, Mame?" shouted the driver.

"We do indeed, Sir. We must not delay; we have a wedding to attend to."

"I'll return us twice as fast as we came, then" replied the driver in jest.

"If you do, then I will pay you twice as much, as long as we return in one piece, "replied Belle, returning his jest.

With the plan of Tobias' return fulfilled, Belle felt overjoyed. She had accomplished something for Ebenezer that he was counting on her for. Her unquestioning commitment to Ebenezer would be cherished by him forever.

Chapter 28

A New Beginning

It was Christmas Eve day, and the city was alive with celebration. There were evergreen garlands and bursts of holly adorning doorways and lamp posts throughout London. A gentle snow fell down on the city leaving a white dusting everywhere and on everything. It was a magical atmosphere.

Most were busy making preparations for the holiday, while others were preparing for quite another celebration, the wedding of Ebenezer Scrooge. It would be witnessed by over a thousand people. The pews were filled from front to back with only standing room left for those who were last to arrive. News of Ebenezer's wedding spread from one end of the city to the other. There were some who had heard about the change in Ebenezer and wanted to catch a glimpse of him for themselves. Some had heard of Ebenezer and Belle's love story and how they had been reunited after forty long years. And, others were there simply as friends and close family wanting to extend their love and support. Everyone had a reason to be there, including all the people whose lives had been touched by Ebenezer in the past year. Mr. Cooper the fruit merchant, Mr. Gordon the fisherman, Mr. Weaver the tailor, and Emily Rose the flower lady were there. Mrs. Harding was well enough to make the journey. Mrs. Nottingham was there with her husband and all her children. Prime Minister Grey and his wife, and Gerald Striker and his wife were also there. The Cratchit family, including Tiny Tim, was there. Even Vicar Wren was there to assist in the ceremony. They were all there.

Ebenezer stood nervously at the altar waiting for the ceremony to begin. He scanned the congregation looking for Tobias. Belle had returned with the good news that he had agreed to come, so Ebenezer expected to find him somewhere in that sea of faces. He looked at each face in each row but he could not find his. Ebenezer couldn't find Tobias, but he was there. He had arrived with Peter. They sat together halfway from the back of the cathedral, and clearly out of sight from where Ebenezer stood.

As the music began, Ebenezer turned to the back of the cathedral. At that very moment, Belle appeared under its grand arched entrance as if she had just descended from the clouds of Heaven. She was a divine beauty. She wore a sapphire and diamond tiara that caught the afternoon sun and cast a brilliant stream of blue and white on the marble columns of St. Paul's. Her gown was made of hand-spun silk with teardrop pearls bordering a high-neck collar of fine patterned lace. Her hair shone like silvered ebony, and her face glowed like an angel's. Ebenezer froze as his bride began her walk toward him. She smiled and winked, putting him at ease. She was the one who had reason to be nervous, not him, for all eyes were on her. She continued walking gracefully toward him as if she were floating on air. She smiled with her eyes at each, and every guest, enjoying this anticipated moment. She had waited a life time for this, and she was going to breathe in every detail and keep it alive from this day forward.

As she approached him, he took her by the hand and they walked up the red carpeted stairs of the altar to join the minister and vicar to exchange their vows. Their vows were spoken to each other with tenderness and respect. When they finished, their souls would be entwined and their hearts would be one forever. Their rings were exchanged as a symbol of their commitment to each other. Their bond of marriage was sealed with a tender kiss. They were now, and forever, husband and wife.

As they turned to face their guests they both threw up their arms in celebration and embraced once more. The crowd replied with a grand applause. The festivities had begun. It was no longer a church ceremony but a gathering of hearts and minds expressing joyful congratulations. No one remained in their seat. As Ebenezer and Belle made their way through the crowd they were stopped by everyone who could reach them. No one was leaving their spot until they had their chance to speak with the couple. With this came the opportunity for the guests to visit and converse with each other as they waited their turn to speak with Ebenezer and Belle.

While in waiting, Tobias struck up a conversation with Peter, who was still sitting next to him.

"Peter, have you kept my desk empty for me when I return?" he asked.

"Mr. Scrooge has given instructions that everything is to remain as is until you have finished your time. How is it there? Are you being treated well?"

"It's not so bad. I suppose it could have been a lot worse and my sentence a lot longer."

"Yes, I do believe so, especially if Mr. Scrooge had reported your first misdemeanor with that rent money."

"Did Uncle Scrooge find out about that?"

"Quite by mistake. He overheard father and me discussing it one day in the office. I had no choice then but to explain everything."

"He didn't make an issue of it with me. He just let it go?"

"Mr. Scrooge is like that. He does a lot of good, and nobody knows about it—just like with your mother."

"What do you mean? She's still in Charing Cross. I'm hoping to visit her before I have to go back."

"Why don't you visit with her here?"

"What are you talking about? Mother's not here."

"You don't know anything about what has happened, do you?"

"Know about what?"

"Eight months back Mr. Scrooge made all the arrangements. He got your mother all set up in his own home, no less. And, Belle has been taking care of her."

"He never let on. All those times he came to see me and I wouldn't talk with him. I was so wrong."

"Ask your mother yourself. She's sitting right up there." Peter pointed up the aisle close to the front altar.

Mrs. Harding was still sitting in the pew where she had sat during the ceremony, talking with the woman seated next to her. Tobias ran to her, dodging guests who were standing and mingling in the centre aisle. He pushed through to her, and embraced her with a kiss on the forehead.

"Mum, me dear mum. I thought you was in the hospital. How did you get here? You look so much better. Oh it's so good to see you."

"Tobias! Let me look at you." Mrs. Harding took Tobias' face between her hands. They hugged each other and wept with joy.

"Thanks to Mr. Scrooge I'm alive and able to look at my son who is standing right here in front of me. Mr. Scrooge has been so good to both of us. We owe him our lives."

"Yes we do, and I need to talk to him. Where is he?" Tobias asked feverishly.

"They are out on the front steps by now getting ready to leave, I'm sure. You'd better hurry if you want to catch him," replied the woman who was sitting with Mrs. Harding.

Tobias ran through the crowd of people, desperately making his way to the front steps where Ebenezer's coach was preparing to drive off. He arrived just as the coach door was closing.

"Uncle, please wait. I must speak with you!" yelled Tobias, climbing on to the sideboard to reach the window of the carriage door. Ebenezer stretched his head out of the window to see him.

"I found out it was you who made all the arrangements for the care of me mother. I'm so grateful for what you've done, but why was I never told?"

"If I had told you when you were in opposition to me, you would have received it as a bribe to regain your devotion. I wanted a genuine reconciliation with you without contrived inducements that is why."

"What I did was wrong. I wanted to tell you, but I was afraid you would reject me and throw me back to the street."

"I will always forgive you, Tobias."

"Thank you, Uncle Ebenezer, I know that now. You've shown me what it is to have a forgiving heart, through all of this that you've done for me and me mum."

As Tobias spoke these words, he began to feel something he had never felt before. It was as if a great burden was lifted off of him. It was the burden of his guilt and shame. He felt free and truly alive. He didn't know it, but it was his heart that had just been transformed. At the very moment this happened, out of nowhere, a long coil of chain links fell into Ebenezer's lap. There must have been thirty or forty links in the chain. Tobias saw it happen but did not believe his eyes.

"Those chains; they appeared out of nowhere. Where'd they come from, and what does it mean?" he asked.

"I believe that an old friend of mine has just been released from a great burden and has received a wonderful gift because of you," replied Ebenezer.

"I don't understand, Uncle."

"You will, son. When we return I will explain everything. For now just ponder this thought: *"There will be no greater reward than to have those who have been changed by your good deeds with you that day in paradise."*

Tobias did not understand what Ebenezer had just said, but he believed that all would be revealed upon his return. Ebenezer now knew that he had accomplished what only he could have for Jacob. He could only imagine what amazing things Jacob would now be able to accomplish for those in need.

With an overwhelming sense of relief, Ebenezer turned his attention back to the one whom he had just given his heart to. The only thing on his mind now was his new bride and the month-long adventure he had planned for her.

"Where are we going, Ebenezer? You will get us back safe, won't you?" asked Belle with a playful tone.

"I will get us back completely safe, with only a few bumps and scratches," replied Ebenezer with a boyish smile.

"Where are you taking me?" insisted Belle.

"Have you ever heard of Zanzibar?"

The End
(for now)